THE SILENCE OF BLEAKRIDGE

The Silence of Bleakridge

a novel by

Michael Lawrence

8N PUBLISHING

First published by 8N Publications, 2024

Cover design: Purpose on Paper
Title page image: Michael Lawrence

Print ISBN: 979-8-9879774-7-7
Ebook ISBN: 979-8-9879774-6-0

What thing better are you, what worse?
What have you to do with the mysteries
Of this ancient place, of my ancient curse?
What place have you in my histories?

From 'Under the Oak', D.H. Lawrence, 1916

'This distinction between past, present and
future is only a stubbornly persistent illusion.'

Albert Einstein, 1955

Framed in my room,
those smiling faces remind me
that I did it.
I took an extravagant idea
pursued it
until it became real.

From 'A Journey', S.J. Lomas, 2021

On the eighth day of November 1899, twenty-six year old Flora Fernsby gave birth to a son, whom she named Morgan. Flora was an energetic casual worker earning a meager living on a smallholding just outside the village of Pendersdell in England's northernmost county, Northumberland. Her son's father was Orson Charles Rainey, soldier turned traveling salesman (door furniture), who wrote poetry and gave readings whenever the opportunity arose. As well as public readings, Orson read privately to Flora on visits to her fragment of the world, but he wasn't with her the day she gave birth, being obliged to attend his wife Gertrude, two hundred and fifty miles to the south in the county of Huntingdonshire, while *she* gave birth, also to a boy.

Gertrude's son was dubbed Roderick Brandon, and surnamed Rainey. Unlike Roderick, Morgan did not initially have a surname as his father was not married to his mother, but three days into his life Flora decided to call him Morgan Rainey and herself Flora Rainey, a change of name that allowed her to pass herself off as a married woman whose husband was away a lot. Although Flora would have liked

Orson to remain with her and Morgan, she wasn't angry with him for staying with Gertrude. Such emotions as resentment and jealousy were alien to her generally cheerful disposition. Orson continued to visit Flora and their son for the entire eighteen months it took his wife to discover, quite by chance, that on those excursions he had not always, as he claimed, been on business and staying with a cousin who lived up that way. She reacted badly to the knowledge, filling his abashed ears with threats of such emasculating retribution that he discontinued his association with Flora and Morgan. However, concerned for their wellbeing, he stumped up for a fifty-year lease on a hilltop farm just outside Pendersdell.

The house on the hill was called Bleakridge.

For some years, Flora made a fair fist of working the farm, but the hill was a hard master that took more out of her than it gave back, and her health suffered, so that she wasn't sorry when Morgan grew sufficiently tall and strong to take over from her, which he did, rather grudgingly, for his was not a light-hearted soul, even then. Light-hearted or not, at the age of twenty-two Morgan took a wife, Sylvia, the village school's assistant teacher, who in the passage of time gave birth to the first of their two children: a son who, from the outset, was called Billy by everyone but his mother.

Bleakridge wasn't a large house, so it was fortunate that Sylvia and Flora got on, sharing a love of poetry, which they would read aloud to the growing lad, a practice which, if he caught them at it, angered his father, working the recalcitrant hill farm week in, week out, developing along the way an extreme distaste for anything even vaguely poetic. Billy was seven when Flora died and he missed her terribly, as did Morgan, though 'missing someone' wasn't something that Morgan would admit to beyond a grunt of affirmation.

By now the school's full-time teacher, Sylvia had no choice but to give up the job she loved in order to take over the running of the house, but she continued to nurture Billy's nascent fondness for the written word, poetry in particular. A stickler for language and usage, Sylvia taught Billy all that she could about ways of expressing himself concisely and effectively on paper, and Billy, ever keen to please his mother, responded well, writing carefully, with considerable expression, until two days before his fourteenth birthday when, following a debilitating bout of influenza in that chilliest of houses, Sylvia too passed away. Following her death, having no one with whom to share his love of writing and reading, Billy became very withdrawn, and – to many, not least his teacher, Mrs. Givens – a surly shuffler, as coarse, as uncouth, as ignorant, as any of the village lads.

The following is Billy Rainey's story.

In part, at least.

1

A four-hour journey, four at least, heading south. He'd almost missed the train. Missed the one before it and dozed while waiting for this one, and when it came almost missed it too. The carriage was stifling, few windows open, harsh sunlight turning scratches on the glass into wounds. He again grew drowsy.

'This seat taken?'

He started. Shook his head almost guiltily. The enquirer put an overnight bag on the rack above and seated himself across the table from him, stretched his legs diagonally, tried to get a conversation going, but he, more inclined toward sleep than inconsequential chat with a stranger, pulled up a newspaper stuffed down the side of his seat. He unfolded it, read the headline: *HITLER ESCAPES EXPLOSION IN BEER CELLAR*. He blinked. Read it again. And again. He sought the date of the paper. *Thursday, November 9, 1939*. He looked out of the sun-grazed window – bland countryside, pre-war housing that gave nothing away – then at the two people in the carriage within his limited angle of view. The sports coat of the man sharing his table was as timeless as his bad toupée. The woman in gray tweed across the aisle was reading what looked like a library book. The cover of the book bore a design that suggested history. He could just make out the title from there without his glasses.

THE VILLAGE THAT DIED FOR ENGLAND
The Unfortunate Fate of Rouklye

Rouklye? Never heard of it. Probably a novel. He didn't read novels.

The interior of the carriage also told him nothing. It wasn't what might be deemed 'modern', but as railway companies didn't update or redesign their carriages very often, that proved nothing. He leaned back. Closed his eyes. Considered the prospect that this was indeed 1939 and that he'd imagined his life. Or dreamed it.

It wouldn't be the first time.

Or the last.

2

That life. That year. As field days go, the second Tuesday of August 2015 was a corker for the British tabloids.

ARTIST CROSSES U.S. CHURCH
A CONDOM TOO FAR!
ART WORLD CRUCIFIXION

The broadsheets were rather more restrained, relegating the story to modest pieces on inside pages, but the rolling TV news looped it all day long. Some reports included the outraged face of Reverend Stoner of The Church of God's Great Light, based in Traverse, Mississippi, who offered a million dollar reward for the life of the artist. 'The bullet of the Lord shall be borne upon the wings of Salvation to the blasphemous heart of Willard Tench!' roared the apoplectic reverend. The work in question, Bones of Golgotha, was a two meter tall scarecrow made of animal bones, filthy rags and used condoms. Its head was a First World War gas mask. A large wooden cross, upside-down, dangled sporran-like from a chain around its waist.

When reporters, photographers and camera crews turned up and virtually camped outside the house in Alpha Road, Will, peeking out through the curtains, said, 'I don't believe this.'

'Well I bloody do,' said Nina. 'I warned you. Just asking for trouble, I said, remember?'

'Shortlisted for the Turner,' he reminded her.

'I can't believe you're actually *proud* of that,' she snapped.

'Not that it stands a chance. Far too pedestrian compared with pickled cows, light bulbs that go on and off, coats draped over chairs. It's just a spot of whimsy anyway. Christians can usually handle stuff like that.'

'Clearly not this Mississippi faction. Now come away from there, *please*!'

It quickly became known as the 'American Fatwa', a joke to many but not to Nina, who agitated for their absence from home until the kerfuffle 'died down' as she put it, generating a laugh from Will, who would have none of it – 'Are you kidding? You can't *buy* publicity like this!' – an attitude that changed the night they returned from an evening with Wendy and Don. No lingering reporters at that time. Always a relief for Nina.

'What the hell?' Will said, pushing at the front door.

Forcing their way in, they found their two year old Labrador, Brancusi, spread-eagled on the inside of the door, throat slit, all four paws nailed to the wood.

Crucified.

Of the two, Will was the quickest to react in any way that might be considered positive. While Nina ranted and wailed he put in a call to the police. A pair of uniforms duly turned up. The female officer was the more affected by what she saw, joining Nina in the kitchen while the PC stared without flinching. 'Not a dog lover meself,' he said.

Fury had taken hold of Will by this time, fury he turned briefly on the copper – briefly because the man was used to householder rage and unwilling to suffer it.

'Don't take it out on me, pal, I'm just responding to the call.'

Will told him of the threat on his life, which rang some bells – 'Oh, that's you, is it?' – after which the PC arranged for Brancusi to be taken away and promised to follow up any leads.

'Not dog leads,' he added, barely suppressing a smirk.

Nina was upstairs when people arrived to take Brancusi away. When she came down she was carrying a bulging suitcase. Will asked nothing, but his question was in his expression.

'You don't seriously think I'm staying here after this, do you?' Nina said.

'So where are you going? Back to Wendy's?'

'I'm getting out of Cambridge.'

'To where?'

'Anywhere.'

'What about me?'

'You?'

'What am I supposed to do?'

'Do whatever you want. Stay here or come with, up to you.'

'I'll get some things.'

3

She waited in the car, engine running. He chucked his bag in the back and climbed into the passenger seat. She was off before he'd fastened his seat belt, hands rigid on the wheel, knuckles white, expression fixed, unreadable. They were some fifteen miles along the A428 when she suddenly screamed, drove a few hundred yards further as the echo of the scream died, and pulled over to the verge, and to a halt.

'What?' Will said.

'What?' she yelled. 'What do you think? What do you *think*!'

'Just sit here a while. Let it all out.'

She didn't let it all out. Merely sat, staring straight ahead. 'This is down to you,' she said at last.

'I know,' he said. 'I know. I don't know what else to tell you.'

She got out of the car. He watched her go round the front, come to his side, open the door.

'You drive,' she said. 'I'm too angry to be safe on the road.'

He got out. 'Drive where?'

'Didn't I already answer that?'

'I don't know, did you?'

'I said anywhere. I don't care. Anywhere, anywhere.'

They switched seats. 'I don't think we should go far while we're like this,' he said.

'While *we're* like this?' she said. 'You seem to be handling it pretty damn well.'

'I don't think it's hit me yet.'

She slapped him round the back of the head. 'Does that help?'

'Nene...' he said plaintively.

'Just drive, goddammit!'

He drove just a few miles, to the forecourt of a hotel on the edge of Huntingdon.

'Hell of a way,' Nina muttered.

'We'll spend the night here. See what the morning brings.'

'I can tell you that now. It'll bring a very strong wish to kill whoever did that to that lovely creature.'

He went into the hotel and took a room for what was left of the night. Returning for their bags, he had to coax her out of the car. Entering the hotel, she didn't look at the receptionist, merely followed Will to the lift.

Next morning she still had little to say other than that she wanted to get as far away from Cambridge as possible.

'Ending up where?' he asked.

'I don't care. I really, *really* don't care.'

The A1 being so convenient, he drove north. Approaching Lincoln, again asking for suggestions, receiving only a noncommittal grunt, he turned west, toward Chesterfield and the Peak District. He stopped the car a couple of times in the National Park, for a break or refreshment, then headed for the Yorkshire Dales, where they spent the night at a small faux olde-worlde tavern. The following morning they went on – always he drove; Nina had no interest in driving, she said – to Carlisle, signs for it at least, at sight of which she said, 'Not there, I don't want a city, *any* city,' and north-east for seventy miles or so, deep into Northumberland, where two things happened in fairly quick succession. The first was that he became exasperated with driving for the sake of it, under her rancorous instruction or to her bitter silence, with no destination in mind. The second was his realization of their proximity to the house he'd seen a few weeks earlier for the first time in twenty-five years. There'd been a For Sale sign at the foot of the hill then, and it was there still, but maybe, he thought, maybe...

'If it's for sale they won't want to rent it out,' Nina said when he mentioned this, 'and if it's empty there won't be any furniture.'

'They might. There might be.'

As it turned out, the house was rentable, on a temporary basis, and the owners – a Mr. and Mrs. Morley – had abandoned most of the furnishings and implements when they moved away for 'family reasons'. Will learnt this from the landlord of the village pub, whom the Morleys had commissioned to show prospective buyers round – something he hadn't needed to do once, there having been no interest in the many months the house had been empty. Through the publican, liaising with the Morleys by phone, Will arranged to rent the place, interior unseen, for a period of three months at a modest rent on the strict understanding that if anyone stepped up to buy it he and Nina would vacate immediately if required.

'Three months?' Nina said when she heard this. She'd stayed in the car during the negotiations. 'I can't stay all the way up here for three months. I have a job. Remember my job? The little thing that pays most of our bills?'

'We don't have to stay that long,' Will said. 'We can leave any time we want. As for your job... extenuating circumstances? The hospital will understand.'

'Not necessarily,' she said.

'Okay, but for now, let's go up to the house we've agreed to rent.'

'*You've* agreed to rent.'

'You could have said no if you'd bothered to shift your arse out of the car,' he said.

'You should have come out and discussed it.'

'Well, it's done now, so let's go.'

'This is going to be a disaster,' she said. 'I know it is, just know it.'

They drove up the track to the house. A track which, until a quarter of a century ago, Will had often climbed alone, sometimes with a friend, and once with Stalin, who was nobody's friend.

4

It was just a shell of a building then, open to the sky, the elements, most of the roof having caved in a decade or so earlier, crashing through the upper floor, between the great oak beams that had supported it for so many years, to become one with the rubble and nettles that carpeted the floor below. Over time, all but two of the windows had been smashed, and the fallen door was a moldering gangplank to an interior which even on the brightest and warmest of days was gloomy and dank. The only evidence of anyone ever having lived there was in the dismembered bits of old utilitarian furniture, an overturned mangle, the stuffing from a shredded horsehair mattress that resembled lumps of mummified flesh. Half fixed, half leaning against one wall, the remains of a wooden staircase teetered upward. Sometimes he would risk the precarious climb, and at the top, crouching within the ribcage of torn and wheezing rafters, gaze up at the open sky and out across the world that encircled the hill as far as any eye could see. At that semi-ruined hovel, nothing could touch him. There he felt powerful, independent, complete. He went there as often as he could, without company if possible.

But that day he was not alone, and he was annoyed. Eric Patchen would have been all right – nearest thing he had to a friend in the village, Eric – but Walter Finch? The local kids called him Stalin because he liked to lord it over the youngsters, push them around, snarl at them. The reason he and Eric were with him today was that Stalin had been at a loose end and demanded their company. They knew better than to argue with Stalin, or refuse him.

The house had been the last place they'd come to. They'd walked and dawdled and tramped for miles in the heat, all the time hoping something worth doing or seeing would turn up. Nothing had. Late in the afternoon they came to the hill and Stalin started up it. Will and Eric had held back, but he'd returned for them, grabbed them by the collar, one in each fist, and hauled them the few steps it took for them to fall in with him. Eric didn't want to go up there because the old house made him uneasy. Will didn't want to go because he preferred to be alone there.

Inside the dull remains of the building a shaft of dusty sunlight spotlighted a section of floor. When Eric pounced on something amid the weeds, Stalin demanded to see it.

'It's only an old belt,' Eric said.

Stalin snatched it off him. 'Soldier's belt,' he said, examining the broad band of coarse khaki, the heavy buckle.

'What would a soldier's belt be doing here?'

Stalin shrugged. 'On leave?' A thought brightened his

eye. 'Deserter, hiding from the MPs.'

'Deserter from what? There's no war on.'

'There's always a war,' Stalin said. 'Troublespots. They get sent all over. Bet he brought a tart up here.'

Will and Eric exchanged glances. Tart?

'Some village bint, Fat Betty or Nora Braden maybe, always up for it, them two. Reckon he brought one of 'em up here, poked her in the dark, couldn't find his belt after, shot off in a hurry.'

'Because the MPs were coming?' Eric said, winking at Will.

'No, 'cos the tart was.' Stalin threw his tongue over his lower lip and panted like a breathless dog.

Will eyed the belt with more interest. It wasn't just a belt now. It was a belt that had belonged to an army deserter who'd shagged a bird here in the dead of night.

He was still inspecting it when Stalin tossed the belt aside in favor of the graffiti on the walls: exploding dicks, hairy fannies, salacious messages and wishes. Fascinated as he was by all this, Stalin's attention was soon drawn to a diseased-looking girlie mag on the floor. He leapt upon it, then stood plying its cum-glued pages apart in the beam of dusty light. Eric craned his neck to see, while Will's eye was caught by something else. He bent over it – a rubber, used and wrinkled – picked it up between finger and thumb, examined it. The teat contained a dry white powder. He imagined it in use, hugging a stiffy inside a female on this very spot. The deserter's stiffy. With his back to the others he tied a knot in the open end and pocketed the thing. (Later, in his room at his grandparents', he examined the condom closely. Sniffed it. It smelt of the house. It must have been there for quite a while for the juice to turn to powder, he thought. He kept the rubber for the rest of that summer, sandwiched like a pressed flower between the pages of a book. The book was *Treasure Island*.)

A suppressed giggle from Eric, who'd stepped away from Stalin, who was rubbing the front of his jeans while ogling the porn mag. Stalin noticed their amusement.

'What's so funny?' He dropped the magazine and took out his penis. 'How's about you giving me a laugh then? Come on, let's see what you two got.'

Eric paled. 'Me mam's expecting me for tea.'

Stalin stroked his tool like a pet. It grew some more. Veins stood out all along it. An unruly brown tuft licked the root. He delved into his jeans, wriggled a bit, cupped his balls with one hand, encircling the shaft with the other, sweeping slowly up and down it. Eric and Will edged toward the doorway, mesmerized but ready to make a run for it if need be. Stalin strolled to the wall and stood before the scribbles, pumping his colossus. A growl started low in his throat, rising slowly to a roar that coincided with the spirited gush that struck the graffiti, burst after burst, and dribbled down and through it. Then Stalin stood motionless, silent, eyes closed. A string of semen swung from the end of his declining prick, thinning and lengthening until it reached the rubble and weeds at his feet. Opening his eyes at last, he cast about for something to wipe himself on, stooped for the soldier's belt, used it, then hurled it up through the void where a roof had once been. Up it went, up and up, before turning earthward again. Will hoped the buckle would smack Stalin on the back of the head as he bent to tuck himself away and zip his fly, but it caught on a beam that ran across where a ceiling had once been, looped it, and swung there, the buckle tap-tapping against the old oak. While Eric wandered outside and Stalin checked the progress of his spunk down the wall, Will watched the belt swinging on the beam. It reminded him of a noose.

5

In 1978, at a Northumbria police auction of goods and chattels held for one reason or another and unclaimed for thirty or more years, a vacationing Missouri insurance actuary by the name of Stanley Singer paid £12 for a plain wooden box containing a cache of handwritten poems on crumpled sheets of paper. Singer bought the box and contents for his wife Grace (not with him this trip as she loathed air travel) because her maiden name – Rainey – was the same as that of the poems' author. Back home in Rocheport, Grace was so delighted with the gift that she had the poems printed in a small private edition entitled *On the Bleak Ridge*, copies of which she presented to relatives, friends and interested acquaintances. Nothing was known about the author of the poems, apart from his address at the time of writing them, and while Grace harbored a small ambition to investigate his background she didn't manage to as, at 3.34 on the afternoon of June 17 1981, she twisted her ankle while stepping off a curb near the home she and Stanley shared with their seventeen year old daughter Alana, and was crushed by a speeding garbage truck.

In July 1985 Alana, now married – to Gus Mildren of Florence, Alabama – had a new edition of the poems made in memory of her mother. Small as the edition was, word got about that its contents were something of a curiosity, and when a local publisher of slim volumes expressed interest in issuing 500 copies under his own logo, Alana accepted. While not achieving anything like international recognition, the collection found an audience large enough for the publisher to print two further editions.

This unexpected if modest success inspired Alana to undertake some research into British people who shared her mother's maiden name. Hoping to find relatives with whom she might correspond with a view to adding branches (or at least twigs) to the Rainey family tree, she was disappointed when only three responded to written approaches, and such vague and cool responses were they that she set the project aside. In the July and August of 1999, however, she and Gus traveled to Europe with their thirteen year old son Evert, visiting several countries, the last but one being England, where she insisted that they go to the southern county of Dorset because a scribbled note found in her late mother's possessions had mentioned a village there, called Rouklye, along with an underlined 'Rainey', which suggested that one or more individuals of that name might once have lived there. While Walter and Evert spent much of the day at the nearby tank museum, Alana went to Rouklye, which she found to her astonishment to be in ruins and under military control.

There were just two unruined buildings in the village, one of which was the 13th century church. On a wall in the church she found a set of boards displaying a number of old photographs of former residents, with notes giving the names of the people in them. One of the pictures was captioned 'Miss L.M. Rainey with son Edward and friend Joey'. A hopeful enquiry of a couple of English people also looking at the photos – a teenage girl and a much older man, her grandfather presumably – added nothing, and that was that as far as British Raineys were concerned.

However, in 2015, when Evert, now 29, announced that he was about to embark upon a touring holiday of Scotland and the north of England, Alana asked him to try and locate the home of the author of the poems her father had bought at auction almost forty years ago. The poet's name was written under most of the titles, while several also contained the words 'Pendersdell, Northumberland'. Only three poems carried the name of his actual house:

Bleakridge.

6

A steep, rough, rattling climb. Approaching the end of it, the yard in front of the house, Nina released her seat belt, and when Will pulled the handbrake before they'd quite stopped, she jerked forward, only just managing not to crack her head on the windscreen. She would have complained, but he was already out, swinging round the bonnet like a big kid. Flinging the passenger door wide with a courtly flourish, idiot grin.

'Madam!'

She slid out. In the shimmering afternoon light the house looked as if it might disappear at a moment's notice. She wished it would, loathing it on sight. Will was already striding toward the front door, fumbling in his pockets for the keys provided by the publican, forgetting that he'd left them in the car. Not finding them, he contented himself with peering through the window to the right of the door. Nina went to the door, inserted the key, let herself in. Preoccupied, babbling a little, he didn't notice until her white cotton top flared like a sudden beacon in the dusky diamond within his hands. He jumped back, startled, then shuffled inside, hands fluttering to casual pockets.

'Thought I'd seen a ghost then.'

'You did, I'm not really here.' She glanced around, muttered, 'If only,' and shivered. 'It's freezing in here.'

'Refreshing,' Will said, 'day like this.' He decided that he didn't think much of the decor but didn't say as much, opting instead for: 'This room used to be bigger.'

'No, you used to be smaller.'

'No, it was, I swear it was.'

He opened a louvre door and peered into a small windowless room, at a pale blue toilet with a black plastic seat – raised – and a bath long enough for your average dwarf at full stretch.

'This has been added,' he said.

'What is it?'

'Bathroom. Didn't used to be a bathroom here.'

'Don't tell me, they used to squat on the side of the hill.'

'There was a privy round the back. Remains of one anyway. But Christ, who in their right mind would put a louvre door on a bathroom?'

'The way the slats are angled you probably can't see in,' Nina said.

He went in. 'You can see out, though. Feel quite vulnerable sitting there, someone moving about outside in full view. And the acoustics!'

'I'll make a point of not listening when you're in there.'

She went through a doorway at the far end of the room,

into a kitchen little larger than the bathroom, with a cream-colored electric cooker of dubious vintage, a big earthenware sink, and an odor of damp, dust and putrefaction, all folded into one. She lifted a metal window catch with her fingertips and snagged a nail. 'Shit.' She slapped the catch. The window jumped open a hand's breadth.

A narrow drawer lined with torn wax paper offered a scattering of cutlery that would have been refused by a charity shop. The drawer was too stiff to close without considerable application, so she left it hanging, turned away, fighting despair. It was all so seedy, so grubby, so... squalid. She turned on a tap – sticky, of course – to wash hands that would wither if not immediately cleansed, and jumped back too late as an explosion of brown water hit the base of the sink, then her. She yelled with fury. Will poked his head in, saw the state of her, the soaked top, clinging, pretty well transparent, improved no end from his point of view by the fact that, as ever, she wasn't wearing a bra, and smirked.

'It's not *funny*!' she said.

'You'd laugh if it happened to me.'

'Not today I wouldn't.'

She shoved past him to the main room, then the front door, and went outside. Will's grin faded. A glossy calendar on the kitchen wall beside a crockery cupboard caught his eye. Color photo of a cute kitten. The kitten represented June, the month the Morleys must have moved out. He flipped through some of the other calendar leaves. A cute kitten for every month of the year. Then he noticed which year. Last.

He heard the car boot slam, then Nina's grunts as she struggled in with her suitcase. He went through to offer assistance, but a sharp look told him to back off. She flung the case on the floor, ripped back the lid, began a demented search for a sweater. Finding the only one she'd packed in her haste, she tore her damp top off and flung it across the room. Her released breasts bounced, and in spite of the situation, atmosphere, mood, Will felt the usual corresponding jump down below and was disappointed when she plunged her head into the sweater, tugged down, and surfaced through the roll neck, shaking out her hair. She glared at him.

'You gonna stand there gawping all day?'

'I was about to gawp upstairs.'

'Why, think it'll be better up there?'

He went outside instead. After the interior gloom the sharp light hurt his weak eyes, bleached the world. Shapes merged, colors shimmered, reconstituted themselves. There seemed to be someone standing by the car. He pulled up sharp, the threat on his life and the horror of Brancusi's fate returning with force. In his bright blindness he saw himself ten seconds on, twitching his last as his blood drained into the earth. He blinked frantically, needing to see his assassin before the deed was done. The shapes and colors reassembled. Nobody there. Trick of the light.

7

'No electricity,' Nina said when he went back in with his bag.

He dropped the bag. 'Probably switched off, place being empty and all.'

'Switched off? Well, that's great, isn't it.'

'Might just be at the mains.'

'And the mains would be...?'

'My guess is the kitchen. I'll take a look in a mo.'

She went there ahead of him, and after some rummaging located the mains in a small damp pantry whose odor flared her nostrils. She flipped the switch. The strip light in the ceiling flickered for a while, then settled down. The small antiquated fridge also struggled grudgingly to life. She looked in the fridge. Half a carton of eggs, squashed pack of soft butter, nothing else. Mould round the door. She left the door open, intending to clear it out later, or tomorrow. Tomorrow! Did she really have to stay here overnight? A succession of nights, days... *weeks?*

'Good, a kettle,' Will said, looking in. 'Put it on, will you?'

'You don't seriously think I'm drinking the water here,'

she said.

'Run the tap for a minute, be all right.'

'You run it, you get drenched and filthy.'

He went to the sink. Turned the cold tap. No explosion this time, but the water was still a little brown.

'Let it run for a bit,' he said again, and left the room.

She shouted after him. 'Tea bags!' Made it sound like an insult.

'Catch!'

A packet came at her. She ducked instinctively. It landed in the sink. She whirled to retrieve it, found the box soaked but the bags inside still dry. The water was running clear now. Irritated that he'd been right about that, she filled the kettle, emptied it, filled it, emptied it, filled it, plugged it in with her eyes half shut, expecting it to blow up in her face. It managed not to.

Will returned with a cardboard box. He dumped it on the scarred rectangle of yellow Formica that served as a worktop. 'You know what we forgot to get on the way?'

'Oh no,' Nina said. 'I can't drink tea without milk.'

'I'll go down to the village.'

He retreated before she could say never mind, I'll get by. This time he made slits of his eyes before stepping into the dazzling light. This high up, above everything, even tree tops, it was like stepping into sky. The first thing he did when he climbed into the car was grab the sunglasses he'd cast aside as he parked. He felt immediately better for the shades. He sat back, hands on the wheel, just breathing. Funny how much easier it is to breathe when you can see properly.

He reached for the ignition. Fumbled nothing. He got out of the car, went back for the keys. As he entered the house he stepped – for a moment – into the Bleakridge of his childhood. The near ruin. But then, a further moment, and all was as it should be, currently.

8

Wherever they went or stayed for more than a few days, Nina moved the furniture. First up this time was the draw-leaf dining table, a heavy old thing that she was intent on repositioning under the main window. She was having quite a struggle, but Will knew better than to interfere beyond an initial offer of assistance (ignored). Kneeling before the brick fireplace arranging kindling and pieces of coal found in the rickety lean-to that stood where the outside privy used to be, he applied a match to twists of brittle old newspaper, also from the lean-to. 'Hope the chimney's not clogged,' he said. 'Wouldn't want to torch the place.'

'Don't give me ideas,' Nina grunted.

Small blue flames battled for life. He leant forward, blew gently on them, and when this seemed to work sat back. Soon the kindling began to crackle. The small flames grew, and warmed up. He felt that he could stay in that position for hours, just gazing into the brightening flames.

'Blast and fuck the sodding bloody thing,' Nina said.

He glanced round. Having managed to get the table to the window she was now struggling with a bow-fronted

1970s sideboard whose legs had caught in the unfitted carpet.

'I did offer to help,' he said. She didn't answer, continued the one-sided struggle. 'Where you trying to put it anyway?'

'Well *I* don't know! Anywhere!'

Which meant anywhere but where it was.

'Why not try giving it a bit of thought first?' he suggested.

'Why not try minding your own fucking business?' she answered mildly.

He got to his feet. Went upstairs. In the bedroom, the larger of two attic rooms – the other being little more than a cupboard – he stood wondering what to do next, what to even think, and coming up with nothing sat down on the three-quarter size bed. There were no covers on the bed, no pillows, just a bare mattress. Tonight they would sleep in their clothes, beneath whatever they could find to keep warm if it seemed clean enough, and tomorrow go off and buy sheets and covers from somewhere or other. Leaning forward from his sitting position on the edge of the mattress he set his chin on the dusty window ledge like a small boy waiting for something to happen. From there, looking out, he could see nothing but strings of light cloud, a bird or three. It was enough. When he went back down the fire was doing nicely and the sideboard was back in its original place. He decided against comment. Nina sniffed herself.

'I stink. I'm going for a strip wash.'

She went into the bathroom, closed the slatted door behind her. When he heard her peeing as if she hadn't closed the door at all, he went outside.

There wasn't room for much of a garden, but the Morleys had attempted one at some point before abandoning it along with the house, today's result being a ragged overgrowth of weeds and grass. The rest was an apron of dry mud and gravel that fanned out at one side to offer standing and turning space for a car or two. Only the frontal boundary was marked by a fence; a fence neither low enough to trip over nor high enough to prevent a drunk tumbling a very long way down.

Will placed a proprietary foot on one of the fence posts and leant on his knee like some 19th century explorer surveying the vast territory beyond and below. The land rose and fell between trees and fields, rivers and roads, churches and houses, scattered villages. Tiny panels glinted as they slid silently across the landscape. Two and a half decades since he'd last stood on this spot. He was seven when his mother cleared off with her Canadian cartoonist, after which his dad took to dumping him on his grandparents in the village down there for most school holidays. His mother's face was a photograph with a crimped corner, his childhood a vague compendium of board games played with his genial, undemanding grandparents. While recalling their cottage as something rather less than chocolate boxy, he felt almost guilty for not lamenting its sacrifice to the bland bungalow that had supplanted it. The cottage, after all, had been as much a part of his childhood as this hill, this view.

Strange how it had happened, the return. Until a few weeks ago he'd had no thought of ever coming back. Driving south on the A1 from Edinburgh, where he'd been participating with little enthusiasm in a pretty dismal art show, he had recognized place names on a signpost and made an impulsive detour. Parking by the pub – The Duck and Whippet – he'd strolled along the main street marveling at how familiar it all was after so many years. At the end of the street, just beyond the church, he'd started along the track that wound up and round the hill, intent on a sight of the old stone house at its summit. He stopped when he saw it, shocked to find that it hadn't remained locked in time for his benefit. No longer a black-eyed ruin open to the skies, it had been restored, not altogether to its advantage. Gazing up at the transformed structure from the comfortable distance of space and decades, he was amused by a rush of delinquent memories, never dreaming that very soon that stinking boyhood haunt would become his adult hidey-hole from holy lunatics with guns.

Today, now, looking down from the property he'd never expected to visit again, let alone occupy, his gaze followed the swoop of a rook to its nest in a confusion of branches over to his left, and from there diagonally to the trees that bordered the early stretch of the track from the the village.

There was someone on the path, a woman, young woman from the shape of her, the way she stood. He couldn't make out her face, but the tilt of her head suggested that she was looking up, toward him or the house. He'd barely become aware of her when he was distracted by a movement on the slope to his right. Glancing that way he saw a boy, also looking in his direction, and was suddenly irritated. What were they gawking at, these people? He closed his eyes to shut them out; counted to ten before opening them again.

Only the boy remained.

9

The boy's name was Colin. Will learnt this when he went down to the pub for a couple of bottles. He'd been chatting to Harry Sewell the publican when the boy came down from the family flat above. Thin dark-eyed kid who looked as if nothing would ever make him laugh. Harry growled at him about something and his son gave Will a look that implied it was his fault. That everything in the world was his fault.

10

Brancusi was out of bounds. A subject never discussed, alluded to, hinted at, but one that often filled their minds, hers particularly. Will might have named the dog, but he'd been hers from a three week old puppy, her choice of pet. Whenever that final image of him returned to her she kicked it away at once, into a small dark box-room of memory with a swiftly bolted door – until the next time it broke out.

They spoke of little else either in the first days at Bleakridge, passing within a hand's breadth of one another, touching only by accident. A couple of times Will reached for her, wanting to give what comfort he could – comfort without reassurance, for there was none – but she pulled back or side-stepped him as though hating the idea of physical contact with him or any other living thing. At some point during these days Will went over what had driven them away. 'Why the dog?' he wondered to himself. A 'You're next' type threat? But why had they, whoever 'they' were, bothered with a warning? Why hadn't they simply waited for him to come in, dealt with him, collected the reward? Bastards who got a kick out of making an intended victim squirm? Maybe. Gradually, while Nina pushed the horror of the dog's demise into the deepest recesses of her mind, he began toying with the idea of using it as a theme for a series of drawings or paintings, and before long was looking forward to the task. He did not embark upon it, however. He couldn't with her there. She'd go berserk.

Late on the morning of day five, Nina went down to the village for the first time, 'to see what the shop has to offer,' she said. As she was setting off, he warned her not to give his name to anyone.

'Why would I even mention you?' she asked.

'Just saying. No one knows who I am here.'

'Not even your pal at the pub?'

'When asked I used your name.'

'You called yourself Nina?'

'Surname. Far as anyone here's concerned we're the Keatings.'

'Ooh, officially a couple at last. Deep joy.'

'And call me Bill down there, not Will.'

'You've never been a Bill,' she said.

'Well, here I am.'

'Have we also got new professions, by any chance?'

'I have. Sort of. Muttered something about writing a book.'

She laughed. 'You, a book? I can't remember when you last even *read* a book. What kind of blockbuster are you pretending to write?'

'No one enquired, so I didn't need to specify.'

'Well, I hope no one asks me.'

'If they do, just be vague.'

'That won't be hard.'

'I had an idea for a novel once,' he said.

'Oh yes?'

'It was about a mountaineer who was scared of heights.'

'Sounds like a real winner.'

'His name was Cliff Edge.'

'It was a comedy?' she asked.

'Dunno. That's as far as I got with it.'

While she was gone he hauled a cast-iron garden table and two matching chairs out of the lean-to and carried them round to the front, the fence at the edge of the yard. He gave the chairs and table the once-over with a damp cloth and shook out a reasonable linen tablecloth found at the bottom of a sideboard drawer. By the time Nina started back, the table was set for the cold lunch he'd prepared. He saw her on the first part of the track, where it passed the bit of woodland known as Slater's Spinney. He continued to watch her until the rising track disappeared behind an extended bump in the lower slopes. How pleasant, he thought, if she smiled at him when she reached the top. He seated himself at the table, bottle of cheap wine and house tumbler to hand, poised to toast the rare event if it occurred. When she joined him there was no smile, no greeting of any kind as she flopped into the chair opposite him.

He eyed the slack shopping bag. 'Not a big haul by the look of it.'

'They didn't have much. Typical village shop.'

'Of course it's typical, Pendersdell's a village, what do you expect?'

'Something more would be nice.'

He stood up. 'I've made some lunch, you hungry?'

She struggled out of her jacket without getting up. 'I'm hot.'

He went inside. She adjusted her hair and sunglasses; folded her arms on the table and sat impassively until he returned with a tray of lunch things.

'Unusual for you, these days,' she said.

'What, lunch?'

She nodded toward the vaguely Neolithic head that he'd been carving out of a block of wood for much of yesterday and part of this morning. This was the first time she'd appeared to notice it, or even the noise he'd made chipping away at it with rusty old tools from the lean-to.

'The mood took me. Might go down and look for more wood later.'

'Down?'

He indicated the spinney far below. Her gaze faltered at the nest-laden treetops.

'I hate them,' she said.

'Hate who? What?'

'Those birds.'

'The rooks? What's wrong with rooks?'

'They make this hideous racket as you approach, then fall silent til you've gone. Eerie. Threatening.'

'It's probably you, making them nervous.'

'I make *them* nervous? They're like lascivious old men. Evil, sharp-eyed old men. Frustrated rapists.'

A small laugh bubbled up. 'Rapists?'

'Watching us. Watching me.'

He tapped the side of the salad bowl. A couple of flies landed on the rim as though invited. He waved them away and, like someone in a trance, Nina dipped into the bowl and ladled salad onto the plate he'd set before her. She was so tense. He would have understood if it was the death threat playing on her mind, but it wasn't that, it was... birds.

'Relax,' he said, pouring wine into her glass, topping up his own. 'Sun's out, we're on top of the world – literally – far from all our worries. Eat! Drink! Be merry!'

She removed her sunglasses and looked at him, very directly. Her eyes were big and round, like a disturbed child's.

'For tomorrow we die?' she said.

11

If anyone had wanted to get in touch with either of them, they would have found it difficult. There was no landline at the house, and Will, hating the idea of being accessible to all, at any time, wherever he was, neither possessed nor wanted a personal phone. Though of similar mind, Nina carried an iPhone for emergences and casual chats, but left it switched off for much of the time. There was one person she'd really felt a need to talk to since their arrival at Bleakridge, however, and that was her sister. She'd tried to phone Wendy from all parts of the house and numerous points on the hill, to no avail.

'This entire hill's a dead zone,' she'd declared after one series of futile attempts. 'Looks like one, is one.'

Only then realizing what she'd been trying to do, Will said: 'Nene. You mustn't use your phone. Mustn't even turn it on. Agents of those holy rollers might have the means to trace us.'

'Trace us?'

'Your phone. Your whereabouts.'

'They're not gunning for *me*,' she snapped.

'No, but...'

He'd let the rest go. Only way to avoid a blazing row.

While Nina's excuse for going down to the village this morning had been to visit the shop, her real reason had been her growing need to communicate with Wendy. She might have kept this to herself if she'd been successful but, annoyed that even there the signal had been so patchy as to break up the most perfunctory attempt at conversation, she let it out over lunch, to which he responded with 'I thought I advised against using your phone.'

She frowned. 'Advised? You're my counselor now?'

'What I'm "counseling" is common sense. Do you want to find an assassin on the doorstep?'

'I wanted to tell Wen that we're all right. She knows about Brancusi, knows we've gone, will be worried sick.'

'There's a phone box near the church. Should be okay to use that.'

'I would have. But guess what. The Out of Order sign in one of the little windows isn't spinning a line.'

Will had made no mention to anyone in Pendersdell of his grandparents having lived there, or of his childhood visits. He wasn't concerned that he might be recognized from newspaper photographs or TV news broadcasts as just one picture of him had been published after the threat, an early self-portrait in which the likeness was far from precise. Initially there'd been a worry that the odd memory might be jogged at sight of him, but twenty-five years is a long time when the starting point is your early teens: his 39 year old face bore little resemblance to that of the 14 year old last deposited here during a school holiday. He half expected to see people he'd once known, hear names from the past, but all but three such individuals seemed to be gone, in one way or another. Of those three, two were retired now. The other, his features much heavier than when last seen, aged seventeen, his voice rougher, conversation just a little less coarse, was Walter Finch – 'Stalin', as was. Walter seemed to practically live in the pub, usually drinking alone while studying some form or reading a paper, occasionally shouting across at someone who'd just come in or said something that he had overheard and decided was worth a comment. If there was one local whose fate Will would like to have known it was Eric Patchen, but he overheard nothing about Eric and didn't dare enquire after him.

While never much of one for chatting with men over drinks in pubs, it was at the Duck and Whippet that he heard a reference to Bleakridge that intrigued him; a casual 'Wouldn't catch me living up there' from Jack Squires – eighty-nine, as he seemed keen to tell everyone – very much a regular at the Duck since his wife died last year.

'You mean it gets a bit blustery sometimes?' Will asked him.

Squires chuckled, just that, and went back to his table with his pint.

'Is that what he means?' Will asked Harry Sewell.

'Oh, it does, specially in winter,' Harry said.

'Does what?'

'Get blustery up there. But he probably meant something else.'

'Such as?'

'Don't ask me, I'm just the bloke behind the bar.'

'Oh, come on,' Will said.

'The Morleys said they weren't sorry to move out,' Harry said. 'Well, I don't know about her so much, but he was in here all the time mumbling about things being changeable up there, all mixed up or something.'

'Changeable? Mixed up? What does that mean?'

'I didn't ask. Might have been talking about the missus for all I know.'

'Weren't you curious?'

A shrug. 'People come here to drink, natter and moan. My job's to serve and listen. Seem to listen anyway.'

'Seem to listen? So if I say tell me more about the house, you say...?'

'Another beer, sir?'

And that was that. He brought the subject up with no one else, so it wasn't until some weeks later, after the Alpha Road murders, when the American came, that he first heard of Billy Rainey.

12

Billy Rainey was useless at everything. Everything people knew about anyway. Few were aware of his love of poetry, the reading and the writing of it. Certainly his teacher, Mrs. Givens, a pinch-nosed, sharp-toned woman, never suspected it. To her, from the day she took over the running of the school from Billy's mother Sylvia he was the brat from the hill – 'the Bleakridge boy' – wretched offspring of an uncouth father given to monosyllabic utterances and gobbing at the ground if he came near you. There was a gleefully circulated piece of tittle-tattle that Morgan Rainey had once rebuffed Mrs. Givens (who was rumored never to have married in spite of calling herself Mrs.), a rejection for which she never forgave him, taking out much of her rancor on his son.

The villagers had never understood what might have drawn Sylvia to Morgan. He was a tenant farmer with little education, small awareness of the world beyond the hill on which he lived, and, as far as they could tell, utterly humorless. If his attributes seemed few to those who didn't know him well, they became few to Sylvia too over time, especially after he began to display a marked dislike for their son from the age of seven or eight. Like his father, Mrs. Givens was slow to find merit in anything Billy said or did, thinking him idle, slovenly and shifty. Having no more liking for his teacher than she had for him, Billy made no attempt to improve his standing with her. Out of school, seeing her coming, he would hunch his shoulders and shuffle by, muttering just loudly enough to be heard sounds that she might consider vulgar or blasphemous. As for his poems, he wouldn't have shown them to Mrs. Givens were she the last overbearing hag on earth.

13

As a ward sister at Addenbrooke's, Nina was efficient and cheerful, liked and respected by staff and patients alike. Several times she had withstood overtures of promotion and the financial lures that accompanied them, shuddering at the thought of becoming a deskbound administrator, preferring, as she always had, to roll up her sleeves on the wards and get in the thick of things. Lately – for at least two years – she'd enjoyed her work far more than her home life, by choice spending more time on night duty than days, thus avoiding Will for precious extra hours, bumping into him more or less in passing, like fellow lodgers, with the merest exchange of words. Occasionally he went away for a day or several days on some art jaunt, and she enjoyed those times most of all. His most recent excursion, to that thing in Edinburgh, had been very good for her as he'd been gone for five days straight, but now she wished that he'd spent those five days at home because a sentimental detour on the way back had resulted in their ending up here these weeks later. All right, she'd been the one who insisted they get out of Cambridge when those swine did what they did to Brancusi, but when they arrived here after their lightning tour of wherever the car happened to be facing, what was her immediate reaction? She should have said, at first sight of the place, 'No, no, anywhere but here,' and dug her heels in. But she'd said nothing. Not a word. Just got out of the car and started moving furniture round. Hourly, she cursed her lack of backbone or gumption or whatever it was, thinking how much longer can I put up with this place, this situation... with Will?

Will had gone off in the car, reacquainting himself with the area for the umpteenth time. Fine with her. Sprawling on cushions in the yard, soaking up the steaming afternoon in her briefs and nothing else, she easily put him out of her mind. Lying there, she felt as brazen as the sky, thinking that if she had to put up with being here she might at least come out of it with a tan. Alone, swathed in sun, eyes closed, for minutes on end she could forget what had brought her here. That and the thought of a religious fanatic or money-driven punk tracking Will here and carrying out the Mississippi commission. The worst part of that was that if an assassin came for him, she would most likely become an associate victim simply by being there. The wisest course would be to make themselves scarcer still. Or maybe that should be make *herself* more scarce. Clear out and leave Will to face it on his own. He'd brought this on them, after all, and the way things had been between them since then she doubted that it would bother him if she left him to it. He was happy here; seemed to be anyway, the idiot. Seemed to feel safe here too. It was only she who worried.

And there was another reason she didn't want to remain here. She missed being active, missed work, her friends, even the ever-changing flow of patients. Some days after their arrival she'd gone to the nearest town and phoned Liz, her line manager, explained everything, been granted generous leave of absence. She'd also phoned Wendy but – wouldn't you know it? – no answer, just a recorded message. Faced with a prompt to leave a message of her own, the best she could manage was a garbled 'Wen, Nene, just... checking in... try again another time,' clicking off in something close to panic, thinking, very nearly simultaneously, 'What the fuck is *wrong* with me?'

A week on from then, with nothing to do but read and sunbathe, she wished she was back in Cambridge. Cambridge, yes; Alpha Road, no. She'd never again be able to open the front door without seeing poor dead Brancusi nailed to the inside of it. If she returned to Cambridge, Wendy would put her up til she found a place of her own. A place for one. Will could do what he liked, stay here for life if he wanted, or as long as it took whoever they might be to locate him and do their thing with him. A pang of guilt at that, which she suppressed, concentrating instead on the delightful prospect of inhabiting her own inviolable space away from him. Their years together had become four or five too many, for her at least. Just short of a decade and a half in one another's pockets and what had they to show? Some reasonable sticks of furniture, a stack of DVDs, CDs, books (mostly hers, mostly replaceable). No kids. Parenthood had rarely appealed. It would have meant giving up her job, for a time at least, surrendering the independence that she valued. Would life with Will have been better if there'd been children? Maybe, maybe not, but sometimes – often – the two of them alone hadn't been enough. Too many instances, days, weeks, with space and time to reflect, speculate, envisage, regret, with no individual to care more about than herself. While primarily her decision, there were times, more of them than she liked to admit, when she felt just a bit short-changed in the 'family' department.

That and one or two others.

14

The warm weather continued. They left the main door open during the day and well into most evenings, hoping to coax the warmth in and tempt it to linger, but it was a determinedly cold house and the temperature improved less than they would have liked. If the owners had installed some form of central heating there might have been a difference, but they hadn't, so there wasn't.

Almost dark now and the door closed. She sat in front of the hearth, the fire they hadn't bothered to light, on a reasonably comfortable easy chair, heels on another, legs stretched out. She wore her only sweater, chin burrowed deep into its high neck, reading glasses constantly slipping down her nose, index finger automatically shoving them up again as she intermittently turned the pages of her paperback, taking very little in. Her mind, now that she'd thought of it, was on that speculative domain of her own, in which everything was beautifully coordinated, where nothing was out of place unless she meant it to be, and waking in a big soft bed, stretching in any direction without fear of being touched or mauled. Also, the luxury of wandering nude around the bedroom, safe from his probing eyes. There was a time when she'd enjoyed him exploring her, but these days she felt uncomfortable like that with him in the room; almost embarrassed. Maybe she would feel differently about new eyes, fresh eyes. Maybe she wouldn't. She didn't often hanker after other flesh against hers, but she was too used to Will to be aroused by the sight or thought of him unclothed. With his waist thickening as his hair thinned, the beginnings of a stoop where he'd been so upright before, eyes less bright than they once had been, there was nothing desirable about him now, or even particularly attractive. Not to her.

She didn't look up when he came in from wherever he'd been, but stared all the more intently at her book.

'Booze!' he said, swinging a bottle from the neck.

She turned a page; made no reply. He stepped closer, shook the bottle between her and the book.

'Yes? No?'

'Not for me.'

'This is the good stuff.'

She glanced up. 'I don't want any.'

He opened the bottle, poured a glass for himself, silently toasted her bowed head, and carried glass and bottle to the table under the window. He sat down. Looked out. There wasn't much to see this far in from the edge of the hill, especially with the day rapidly ending. A few twitchy pinholes struggling through the darkening fabric of the sky, no moon. The silence creaked behind him. He fought a sigh.

Silence would have been fine if he'd been alone, but he wasn't alone and the barricades were getting higher. Soon be insurmountable. As the last of the day's light dissolved, his reflection in the glass established itself, transforming his unremarkably angular face. Hair swept back, eyes a tiny gleam in cavernous sockets, unshaven jaw a depthless black. In the glass he looked younger by ten or twelve years, like a studious terrorist.

Ten or twelve years.

Twelve years ago he'd been an archaeological illustrator producing drawings of excavated artifacts and reconstructions based on limited source material. It wasn't an overcrowded profession, so there was a fair bit of work for a freelance, but the pay was poor, and with Nina's staff nurse salary their only other income they hadn't lived it up much. Hadn't often wanted to. They'd liked being together then, had needed few others and little else. Their silences were companionable. But with a series of cutbacks in archaeological research, the commissions had dried up and he'd been forced to take whatever work he could, a succession of dull jobs that culminated in temporary employment as general dogsbody and laborer with a stonemason. It was during his time there, while holidaying in Italy with Nina, that a chance meeting changed everything, for him if not her. Returning with an unexpected enthusiasm for the properties and possibilities of stone charmed the mason, Ted Slomis, into letting him try his hand at working with it – and he proved a natural. Couldn't put a chisel wrong. When the job eventually folded, he built a rudimentary studio at the back of the house and had blocks of stone delivered on which to develop ideas that were by then coming thick and fast. Nina, almost as fascinated by his progress as he, was at his side when he entered the most exhilarating period of his life, encouraging him in his every experiment, urging him on when doubt overcame him, suggesting areas of innovation when he felt he was becoming repetitive or predictable.

Years on from that time, gazing at the terrorist in the black glass, he recalled that old passion, and life with Nina then. Over his shoulder, within the reflected room, tonight's Nina, four months shy of forty, sat reading by the unlit fire while the young Nina of memory flew about the room like a hyperactive Pre-Raphaelite nymph. All that lustrous hair, a shade brighter than auburn, so long then, so full. As always, the present day had the stronger pull, and spry young Nina, vivacious Nina, danced away into the night while the woman she'd become, waspish of tongue, formidable in her silences, shifted in her chair. Soon she would close her book and go upstairs, and some time later ritual would send him after her. He would climb in beside her and they would lie side by side or with their backs to one another like strangers sharing a bed by accident.

Some nights, usually around 3:00 a.m., he would wake suddenly, struggle for a moment to make sense of the little attic room with its sloping ceiling and low walls, and realize that he needed a pee. He would slide out of bed and pick his way down the narrow staircase. Sometimes, wide awake after the trip to the bathroom, he would remain downstairs for a while, sipping something, drawing perhaps, but more often than not immediately go back up, slip in beside a Nina disgruntled by the sudden tilt of the mattress, and lie longing for sleep to reclaim him. He hated waking in the night. Night was when the whispers came. The terrifying rumors of mortality that would spin him endlessly until the window lightened, whereupon, safe once more, he would fall asleep, exhausted.

15

Billy had lived at Bleakridge all his life. When he was very young Granny Flo had the main upstairs room, the bedroom-loft she called it. The only other room up there was too small even for a child's bed, and was therefore used for storing all the household things that had no place or use elsewhere. With no other bedrooms available, he and his little sister Sal and their parents slept downstairs, on two mattresses on the floor. In his lifetime a family of five initially, little Sal caught a cold one Boxing Day and never shook it off until she couldn't breathe any more; then, when Billy was seven, Granny Flo died. While he'd missed Granny Flo tremendously, her absence meant that his mother and father could move into the bedroom-loft, leaving him with the ground floor all to himself at night.

His father, Morgan, was a generally dour man, surly and unforgiving, but Mama... Mama, it was she who made his life worth living, she who loved him and introduced him to poetry. Sylvia was fond of Blake, Shelley, Keats and their like, though her favorite was the countryman, John Clare. While Billy was still quite young she obtained cheap volumes of their works from the market – old copies mostly, tattered, well-thumbed – and read them to him at bedtime; other times too. It was the way she read them, with such quiet relish, that gave him the idea of writing some poems himself, just for her, and he did, and Mama always asked for more.

Sylvia died in 1940, about a year into what became known as the Second World War, her death a far more traumatic event for Billy than the war itself, which in any case barely touched Bleakridge and Pendersdell. It was war poetry, reading it, poem after poem after poem, that helped him get beyond that year, alone with his now virtually silent father; poems of the first war, the so-called Great War, by young men who'd either died in it or experienced it and survived it: Gurney, Sassoon, Owen, Rosenberg and others. He envied their having such a cause to write about, such extremes and trials, and began to dream of writing about the current war as that generation of poets had theirs.

The war was still going strong when he turned eighteen and was called up. His initial excitement at the thought of the experiences he might describe as a soldier quickly faded, however, for instead of being immediately ordered off to war he was sent to a Dorset valley recently commandeered by the War Office – at the expense of its two hundred and twenty or so residents, turfed out to find accommodation elsewhere – for weapons testing and troop training. There, he was billeted with twenty-three other conscripts in one of the valley's woods, their accommodation a tunnel-shaped hut made of corrugated steel and iron.

From the outset it was clear that he had little in common with the other young men, many of whom had loud voices, an ugly sense of humor, appalling habits. The food wasn't much cop either, but that was just one of the things you had to put up with. Things such as prolonged physical exercises, endless rifle drills, the loading, unloading and cleaning of weapons, learning how to use bayonets and hand grenades, camping out in all weathers without any kind of cover, queuing for inoculation against previously unheard-of diseases, and marching, marching, marching. Many of the conscripts seethed about having to do all these things in this damn valley when they could be abroad, fighting those kraut bastards, killing the buggers.

The wood in which Billy's hut was situated was a five minute walk from a village where families had lived for generations but where no one lived now, by order of the government. There, great coils of barbed wire had been left wherever they'd come to rest, along with discarded parts and bits of Army vehicles. In the gardens there were barrels, boxes, bottles and all sorts of other detritus. Already it was hard to imagine the place as it must have been before. No tanks then, no lorries and jeeps, men shouting and being shouted at, no explosions, guns firing, camp fires built too near properties to be safe. One cottage had been burnt very nearly to its foundations shortly before Billy's unit arrived. Many of the front doors had been locked by the residents when they were ordered out – locked because they expected to be allowed to return when the war was over – but the locks hadn't held, and the chairs and beds had been a real gift to doze upon, play dice on, have a bit of fun in with a girl if you could find one willing enough. There'd been official warnings:

'Treat these properties like they were your own!'

'But sir, we do.'

Still, amid all this, surrounded by it, Billy found things to write about. Poems. Many poems, about the war as viewed from afar, about the camp he was billeted in and the people in it, about the daily grind and the repetition of tasks that seemed pointless the first time around, let alone the fiftieth. It wasn't stirring material like running across battlefields with a bayonet attached to your rifle, of the mud of rain-sodden trenches at night, of festering wounds and dead comrades at your side, but it was all that presented itself to him – except when he used his imagination. When he let his imagination take flight entire worlds of conflict, pain, fear and endurance opened up in the form of poems. A young man's poems. Naive young man's perhaps, but poems nevertheless.

16

There wasn't even the distraction of a television or radio at Bleakridge – two items the Morleys had not left behind. Even if she'd had her laptop, with no broadband it would have been useless as a communication tool. The lack of such means brought the place in around her, like a slowly collapsing tent, and she'd taken to going out in the car more frequently to experience different things, however commonplace those differences might be. She was used to the bustle of the wards, conversation, laughter, the sound of people moving about. Even on night shift, the quietest hours, there was a murmur of something. And the streets. She missed the streets of Cambridge, the shopping centers, arcades, bridges, the noises and sounds you gave little thought to, barely noticed, so used to them were you. And their house. Even when the TV and radio were off, no music playing, no one speaking, it never seemed so quiet that you wanted to shout to fracture it. Always, there was a whisper or hint of something. But at Bleakridge, nothing. Ever. A plane going over was quite an event. Such a rarity aside, you had to cross the yard to the fence to hear the slightest sound – the rasp of one of those damn rooks down in the spinney, the very distant hum of traffic – but in the house you didn't even get that. The silence of Bleakridge was so absolute that after a drive out she dreaded returning to it. Twice now, she'd stopped the car low down on the track, just sat there – 'A minute or two, that's all, just a minute' – before continuing on, up, into the yard, to enter the house sour of mood and countenance, hating everything about the place; despising Will for dragging her there, for bringing this godawful situation upon them.

Today, more overcast than other days of late, she hadn't taken the car or gone far, just part way down the hill, not on the track, on the hillside itself, picking her way down the tussocky uneven ground. She was about a third of the way down when a sharp buzzing sound startled her, causing her foot to slip and pull the rest of her after it. Too shaken for a moment to think what the sound might be, she realized, sat up, tugged her phone out, found that she'd forgotten to turn it off after her last failed attempt to use it locally, and that a text had come through. She glanced about her. Laughed in spite of the pain in her backside. Was this the one tiny part of the entire godforsaken hill that a phone signal could be had? The *only* part?

The text was from her sister. 'This is written in the unlikely event that you'll get it given your lack of signal, but you didn't give me an address to write to, so here's hoping.' Wendy went on to say that she'd given Don his marching orders. 'About bloody time,' Nina said aloud. She despised without quite disliking Don. Don was hard to dislike. He and Wendy had been married for eighteen years, during which time she'd found evidence of his involvement with a number of women. After each discovery there'd been furious recriminations from her and groveling apologies from him coupled with assurances that it wouldn't happen again, which always concluded with her being won over and forgiving him. Often over the years Will had been the first to hear of Don's dalliances, from him personally, usually mentioning them to Nina who, though outraged, had kept them to herself rather than upset her sister. Don's main requirement of his side-order partners seemed to be that as he grew older they grew ever younger, as if to achieve some sort of balance. According to today's text, Don's most recently discovered liaison was with a girl of sixteen, a demographic too far even for the long-suffering Wendy, who had decided that Becky and David, both older than this latest conquest, could get by without such a father. Don had been told to pack his bags, and had done so, with great reluctance and genuine sorrow. At the end of the fairly extensive message, Nina laughed to find that Wendy had included the address of Don's new digs in case she or Will wanted to keep in touch with him. 'You might,' she said later, showing this to Will. 'I sure as hell don't.'

Wendy had always considered Nina fortunate in that Will, unlike Don, didn't play around. What she didn't know was that Will could do nothing right for her sister these days: a detail that Nina hadn't felt a need to share. It had been bad enough before the ridiculous flight from Cambridge, but here, on this damned hill, she couldn't stand the way he hung up his clothes or laid a table or shut a door or sat in a chair. Even his speaking voice grated now, and when he came into a room it felt as if he drew the walls in with him, imprisoning her even more in this dreadful hovel he'd brought her to.

17

Billy didn't mix much with the others. Some thought him odd because he didn't engage in sweary talk or bawdy singsongs or loudly fantasize about fucking and being sucked off and all. A few made fun of him for keeping to himself, especially when sitting alone, writing in the notebook he always carried. A few said 'Whotcha writing, pal?', to which he might offer a shrug, or mutter something like 'just writing'. One, a swaggering loudmouth named Cranton was more intrusive and scathing than the rest, with 'Writing to Mummy, are we?' sort of comments. The first time he said this Billy kept his head down and made no response. The second time, Cranton said 'He's writing home to Mum again, boo-hoo, Mummy, Mummy, wish you was 'ere to tuck me in.' Again Billy said nothing. Merely set aside his notebook and stared at a wall. He gave a similar response the next couple of times too.

It was the fifth time that did it.

He was on his own in one of the abandoned cottages of the row where they said the post office used to be, trying to write a poem about life back on the hill. He'd never had much love for the hill, or the house, but it had been home all his life, all he knew of the world really, and being so far from it, in such company and accommodation, he was surprised to find that he missed it. Missed *it*? No, not really. Jess. He missed Jess. He didn't miss his father, who he knew would only miss him for the help he had no choice but to give, working the lousy hill.

The room he sat in was a mess. Ornaments and pieces of furniture had been smuggled out and sold in neighboring villages or at auction – not officially but for the profit of individuals – and what remained had been mostly smashed up or pissed on. An old oak table had been pushed over, onto its side, one leg lying on the floor by his feet. He'd picked the table leg up when he sat down to write, but quickly put it down again, thinking: *Someone's home, once.* He sat on the better end of a couch that had been jumped on, a rip in the material at the other end exposing stuffing and springs. The light that came through the window was early evening's, fading but adequate for crafting a few lines. The door hung open, having been kicked back by an Army boot some days ago. When Cranton and a pair of cronies strolled by, off-duty like Billy but unlike him in need of entertainment, Cranton, seeing him there, head bowed over his notebook, sauntered in, all shoulder-roll and smirk.

'Still writing to dear old Mum, are we, Rainey?'

Billy stopped writing in the middle of a line that would never be finished. Stopped, but did not look up after the single glance that identified the speaker, the hand holding the pencil no longer moving while Cranton embarked on another coochie-coo-mummy's-boy routine, and it washed over him: his life – his innocent, trusting life – up to the devastating point at which his mother died, and he put away the notebook and got up, not looking at Canton, intending to walk past him, find solitude again, elsewhere; but Cranton stepped to one side, blocking the way out while still smirking and uttering his inane taunts, and Billy reached down and gripped the heavy table leg, and lifted it, and brought it round and down, silencing his tormentor with a single blow, walking past Cranton as he fell, barely noticing the other two as they stepped aside, astonished, to let him through.

There was no subsequent retribution. The hospitalized Cranton was asked what happened, but he couldn't speak yet as his nose had been broken and his lips were swollen. One of his mates said he'd tripped over some rubble in the village street. The explanation was accepted and after that no one commented on Billy's writing or solitude, even Cranton when he got his speech back, obliged to accept the fact that his nose would never be the same again. He glared at Billy often, unless Billy looked at him: then he would glance away, or pretend to be interested in something or someone else.

18

She was in the main room, the 'living room', ha-ha, pottering for the sake of it, trying to overcome boredom and failing, when she heard the car. She rushed to the bathroom, turned the light on, locked the door, and sat on the downed lid of the toilet to await his shadow on the louvre slats. The shadow duly fell, hung there for several breaths, and moved on. For a full minute she heard neither sound nor movement. Imagined him lurking somewhere beyond the door listening for her as she was listening for him. Eventually, realizing how stupid this was, she flushed the toilet and ran water briefly into the basin. She was reaching for the door catch when the ceiling light flickered and died. In the slatted semi-dark she tugged the light cord once, twice, three times. The light did not come back on. She opened the door. Will wasn't there and the house was quite still, quite silent. Rush of panic now. Suppose it hadn't been him? Suppose it had been someone else? Some stranger? Some *armed* stranger? Suddenly every inch of the house was loaded with Threat.

She hastened to the kitchen. No one there. She leaned

up the stairs. No intruder's shadow. Finally – obvious once she thought of it – she went to the main door. Their car stood outside. Will was struggling to get something out of the boot. While not particularly pleased to see him, she found herself breathless with relief, and joined him.

'What's that?'

'What's it look like?'

It looked like part of an uprooted tree stump shorn of most of its roots.

'What's it for?'

'Thought I'd carve something out of it.'

'How did you get it in there?'

'Steroids. Which seem to have run their course. Give us a hand.'

'The bathroom light's gone,' she said.

'Gone?'

'Ceased to function.'

'Help me with this, will you?'

She hesitated before: 'And put it where?'

'Inside. Can't leave it out here, might rain in the night, I want it dry.'

'It's already hideous enough in there without half a tree.'

'Well, as you've so often said, it's not exactly home.'

'I'll have to go and change.'

'Change?'

'You don't think I'm lugging that about in these, do you?'

She was wearing white dungarees, but he wasn't

persuaded. 'It'll only take a minute,' he said.

'Time has nothing to do with it, I'm going to change.'

'Ah, don't bother!'

He hauled the stump onto the rim of the boot, from where he let it fall to the ground, jumping clear just in time, as did she. Then he dropped to one knee and encircled it with his arms, prepared to lift it.

'All I'm asking is that you hang on til I change into something *else*,' she said.

He looked up at her. 'It's all right. Forget it.'

'Fine. Consider it forgotten.'

She stalked back to the house, and inside turned round, completely round, twice, the heels of her palms pressed against her temples, screaming silently.

There was a yell from outside. Her name.

'Oh, fuck off,' she muttered.

A repeated shout. 'Nina!'

'What!'

'My back!'

She returned to the door. He was sitting on the ground leaning against his horrible hunk of wood, face contorted.

'My back's gone,' he said pathetically.

'Serves you right, should have waited.'

'I'm in agony!'

She crossed the yard. 'Where does it hurt?'

'My fucking back, I told you.'

'Whereabouts in your fucking back?'

'Lumbar, as usual. I can't move.'

She stood looking down at him.

'What do you want me to do about it?'

'Well, I don't know. Your province.'

'I'm not a physiotherapist.'

'Help me!' he pleaded, regardless.

It wasn't easy, but she managed to get him indoors. He protested all the way. She deposited him in one of the armchairs, where he half sat, half lay, groaning. She made a move toward the kitchen.

'Where you going?' Almost hysterical demand of her retreating back: *Don't leave me alone, I'm in pain.*

She turned in the doorway. 'I'm putting the kettle on.'

'The kettle? What about me?'

'What about you?'

'My fucking back!'

'Rest it.'

She went through.

'There must be *something* you can do!' he yelled after her.

Her disembodied voice wafted lightly. 'You could have slipped a disc for all I know. I know nothing about slipped discs.'

He stared at nothing. 'Slipped disc?'

'But it's probably just a pulled muscle.'

'If you don't think it's a slipped disc, why say it might be?'

She came back in. Stood before him, arms folded.

'I'm going to try a hot compress. Hence the kettle. When the muscles have relaxed sufficiently I'll give you a spot of gentle massage. No guarantees, but it might help.'

'Why didn't you say that in the first place?'

'Now there's a tough one,' she said, and returned to the kitchen.

19

Evening. Needing a break from the chatter and coarseness of the others, Billy, still in uniform, jacket unbuttoned, strolled into one of the woods bordering the abandoned village. There, the soft air held threads of wild garlic and early thistle. Amid the trees he saw cottages, unoccupied for less than four months, that already showed signs of wear and neglect. Walking slowly, glad to be alone, he heard a curious sound – penny whistle or flute, something of the sort – gentle, wistful, ethereal even, and made his way in the direction from which it seemed to come. But as he progressed the music ceased, all at once, bringing him to a simultaneous halt yards from a house more ramshackle than most, and in the silence, while he considered what to do next, where to go, a line came to him, a line which, by its very existence in his mind, craved companions. Wishing to conjure those lines while the first was still fresh, he picked his way through waist-high grasses and between a host of malevolent brambles massed before the house. Clear of these guardians, he found all but one of the windows on this side of the building broken or badly cracked. The unbroken one was on the upper floor. Passing through an entrance whose battered door lolled inward, held in approximate place by a single hinge, he stood in what once had been a living room. While the rest of the recently-vacated properties of the village and valley were not yet uninhabitable, this one hadn't been lived in for years going by its empty, soot-blackened fireplace, the ivy crawling through ragged rectangles of the former windows, around which old curtains hung in tatters.

It was so still in there, still and silent, utterly silent, as if the walls themselves had shut the world out. The air, slightly moldy, smelt as if it hadn't shifted or been disturbed for an age. There was still some furniture, battered, very dusty: a dining table and awkwardly-placed chairs, a couch with a deep hollow at one end where a heavy person must have sat for extended periods, a couple of threadbare easy chairs, a bland old sideboard. A carpet, so grubby that it might have been trudged across repeatedly by muddy boots, sprawled, rucked up and torn here and there, small weeds and nettles struggling to push through, and expand. There were cobwebs too – some very large, drooping like shawls from high corners – and the faded wallpaper, innocuously-patterned, was peeling in places, while the off-white ceiling was so badly cracked that it looked as if might cave in very soon.

Moving further into the room he saw the foot of a staircase that twisted upward behind an ascending wall. The uncarpeted stairs, the set and rawness of them, reminded him of the stairs at home, and once that comparison was made his mind filled with life as it had been at Bleakridge when Mama was there, comforting him when he felt a bit low, tending him when he was sick, feeding him, reading to him, encouraging him when he'd attempted to write lines of his own. Now there was only his father, just the two of them, and they'd never really got on when alone together; had got on even less well since Mama's passing.

Billy sighed, and returned his mind to the line that he'd wanted to write down to see where it led, and hesitantly, feeling like an interloper, an intruder, seated himself on one of the dusty dining chairs, took out his notebook and one of the three pencils he always carried in a pocket of his jacket. Now that he was close to it he noticed cutlery on the table, old cutlery, well-worn, knives and forks, spoons, just tossed there or so it seemed. Glancing round once more, he saw some graffiti on a bit of wall where the wallpaper had partially unpeeled: all the usual stuff – crude rhymes, innuendo, swear words, dates, names, genitalia – which suggested for a moment that squaddies had been here, a quickly-dismissed conclusion as the graffiti looked as if it had been there for some years. A previous generation's work? If so, they weren't any kinder or purer than people are now. As if to consolidate this assumption, the room darkened – a cloud passing over the little sunshine that had managed to slip through the foliage outside – and he bowed his head and wrote that first line, and, after the briefest pause, a second, a third...

We each took a step backward
As though quitting a circle
We'd been caught occupying by mistake

... but then paused, unsure how to develop whatever theme the lines might suggest, and in the pause heard again the faint sound that had brought him here, a flute or tin whistle or some other kind of pipe. Alarmed to think that he wasn't alone here, he got up, intending to leave, but as he did so the music again stopped abruptly, as if to discourage his departure. He relaxed a little then, and as he did so a shaft of bright light entered the room by way of one of the broken windows and fell upon the graffiti wall, directing his gaze in particular to a drawing of a man hanging by the neck from a gibbet. Curiously, once focused on the drawing he found that he couldn't easily look away, and while he looked, random thoughts flittered like agitated bats in his mind, triggering a reflexive hand movement that brushed some of the cutlery on the table. Looking down, finding that he was touching a particularly pointed knife, he decided to commemorate his presence here. Getting to his feet he found a sufficiently unsullied patch in the old plaster and began to scratch his first name – not Billy but his given name, which his mother always called him by – but when this was done he paused. Just the one name or...? No. All of it. He suddenly wanted to make it plain that William Rainey had been here. He'd barely started the first letter of his surname, however, when –

'What the fuck you think you're doing?'

He jumped, dropping the knife, whose point only just missed his foot.

'I said what the fuck?' the voice said again.

He turned. Two steps up from the foot of the staircase: a lad, a couple of years younger than him perhaps, lanky, wild-haired, angry. In one hand he held the pair of flutelike pipes he'd been playing.

'I...,' Billy stammered. 'I...'

The lad started toward him, stuffing the pipes into a side pocket of his jacket. 'What this time?' he said, reaching him and leaning forward to peer at what he'd started to write on the wall.

'Just my name,' Billy said, as embarrassed as if he'd been caught writing something smutty. 'I didn't mean any harm. I was just... just...'

'Just-just, just-just,' the boy mocked. 'It's not your house to just-just do stuff to.'

'But no one lives here.'

'Not now they don't. Used to. Before you lot. It was mine then.'

'Yours? You lived here?' The other merely grunted. When he added nothing more but continued to peer at the wall, Billy, attempting to sound bolder than he felt, said: 'I don't think you should be here now.'

The youth turned his head. His eyes were gray, and

alarmingly pale to Billy, in that light, that place.

'It's where I would be, if we hadn't been booted out by you fuckers.'

'Not by me,' Billy said.

'You're one of 'em.'

'I was conscripted.'

'What?'

'Called up. Sent here for training. I don't want to be here, I want to be back home.'

At this the boy's shoulders sagged. He turned away, to gaze at nothing visible. 'Home,' he said quietly.

Billy waited for more and when nothing came, said, 'I'll be off now,' but he'd taken no more than a step when the boy spoke again.

'Vandals. Vandals in uniform. Smash windows, jump on furniture, shit in bedrooms, wreck everything, even the church. A shell went through the church roof last month.'

'I heard about that,' Billy said. 'Accident, they say.'

'Doors kicked in. Locked, most of 'em when everyone left, now just lying there, broken.'

'I didn't do any of that. I wouldn't. Other folk's homes.'

The boy indicated the name Billy had half carved. 'You don't seem bothered about this one.'

'It didn't look like anyone had lived here for years,' he said. 'And all this other stuff, here already, so I thought...'

'That you'd add your name to it, yeah, right.' He again looked at Billy's inscription. 'William,' he read. 'What else were you going to put?'

'My surname. Rainey. Just that.'

'Rainey?'

Billy shrugged.

The boy frowned at him. 'Your name's Rainey?'

Billy shrugged again.

'You know anyone else named Rainey that lived here?'

'Here?'

'In the village.'

'Was there someone here named Rainey?' Billy asked.

The youth grinned suddenly, broadly, all teeth. 'A Rainey in uniform,' he said. 'Here! Priceless. Priceless.' ˙

But his amusement dissolved almost at once.

'I'm away,' he said, 'before your security sods catch me.' He went to the open doorway, leaned out, listened, then looked back. 'Nothing else on that wall, right?' Billy said nothing. Just stood. 'Better not,' the boy said. 'I know you now. Your name.'

With this he slipped out of the house, into the woods, to return by some route known only to himself, to wherever he lived these days. Billy waited a minute before he too left. Starting back the way he'd come, after a few steps he paused; then, on impulse, headed in another direction in order to avoid returning sooner than he must to the hut he shared

---

˙ To hear all about the Rainey who used to live in that recently evacuated village, see 'This Ruined Place', published by 8N Publishing.

with his loud and coarse compatriots.

Distracted and a little disturbed by the encounter in the old house, he walked less carefully than he should, not always along the tracks officially described as safe. While the landmine he trod on didn't blow him to smithereens, it caused sufficient injury for him to be invalided out of the Army, labeled 'unfit for service', and sent home. His subsequent limp, plus the scar generated by a gash in his left temple where he fell on an exposed tree root, completed the image of the wounded soldier. A good result, he might have thought on the train, if his leg wasn't so damn painful, and if Mama had been there to greet him, welcome him, hold him in her loving embrace.

When he got home, after limping the three mile walk from the station and climbing the hill, he found the house in darkness, learning subsequently that some weeks earlier his father had collapsed on the side of the hill while working and faded away all but physically, to be eventually discovered by a villager glancing up and carted away, buried in the churchyard with little ceremony, no genuine mourners.

Billy was alone at Bleakridge now. Just him there. Him and the shadows. The stillness. The silence.

20

The lump of wood that Will had brought up by car hadn't made it into the house. He worked on it in the yard. At night he covered it with tarpaulin in case it rained. A figure of sorts soon emerged, a gnarled, crouching, malformed figure that Nina didn't care for at all. Nor did she like where he placed it when it was finished. Already imagining assassins behind every rock, in every shadow, one thing she didn't need when she opened the door or drew the curtains first thing was a menacing effigy glaring at her from the yard.

One night she looked out and, in the light of a high, bright moon, thought for a second that there were two huddled figures there, staring at her. She very nearly passed out.

21

One wet and stormy night shortly after her twelfth birthday, Ella's mum and dad left her at home while they popped out for a drink, like they always did on Friday nights. Bad Friday, that one. A long steep skid off a hillside road, and suddenly, unexpectedly, she was an orphan. A few weeks later her only surviving relative, Auntie Joan, brought her to live with her in her rented cottage just outside Pendersdell village.

By the time she was fourteen, Ella stirred every lad for miles around. The way she looked, walked, disported herself. It was her proud boast that she was named after a famous Hollywood film star. It didn't matter that no one had heard of a star called Ella Raines or seen anything she'd been in; the association made their Ella a bit of a star too. Ella played on this, and the lads loved it. They were all over her. Hung around her every chance they got.

Ella at eighteen, though. At eighteen, Ella was as tall as many a young man, and very striking, with luminous green eyes, a mass of flying titian hair, a laughing mouth that filled lads' dreams. Wet dreams, often. Billy's dreams too, when he first saw her on returning home, though you'd never know it from the way he avoided her, never met her eye; even, sometimes, turning about and going back the way he'd come rather than meet her face to face.

22

As well as hacking away at odd bits of wood, Will had made a fair number of drawings. Most of them were done away from the house, on this or that walk. Sometimes he went further afield, in the car, but in the main he concentrated on the immediate vicinity. They weren't great drawings, he didn't need anyone to tell him that, but he was out of practice. Years out of practice.

Today it was too hot to draw, do anything much at all, so he lolled in the old deckchair he'd dug out of the lean-to while Nina, sick of merely sunbathing, tore into an overgrown patch of weeds near the fence. The chair's faded canvas smelt musty and earthy, just short of moldy, but he was soon sufficiently used to it not to notice. Stripped to his underpants, the sun heating his skin, he drifted in and out of a sticky doze. Between these leisurely excursions he focused hazily on Nina, all-foured in the weeds. Dressed as skimpily as him, her aquamarine briefs beautifully complemented her glowing brown skin. Coming out of the latest dip into semi-consciousness, he tugged down the rim of his hat and watched her from its shadow: the way she reached and tugged at the weeds – 'Gardening to stop myself going right over the edge with boredom,' she said of this – troweled with sharp stabbing movements, shuffled on her knees this way and that on the dry earth. With the sun more or less behind her she might have been twenty-six again, the age she was when they met.

She'd been using her annual leave from the Central Middlesex to help with the excavations of a Roman villa near Winchester and he was one of the paid assistants. She caught his eye at once, and not just his. When actively engrossed, she had a way about her that quickened the pulse of every man or youth on the site. She wore more then, of course, but it was another hot summer and shorts and T-shirts were standard attire, worn spectacularly by her, that bright cascading mane of hair seeming to have a life of its own as she reached and gathered, her back arching and hollowing, long thighs tautening, relaxing.

Nina at twenty-six. Jesus.

But the older woman viewed from the shadow of his hat compared favorably with the younger. The differences were fine with him: a little extra round the waist, a softening of the belly, a rounding out rather than a slackening of the breasts, hair a bit shorter, the odd strand of gray that she was happy not to disguise. She might have worn more on the Winchester dig, but these years later, up on this hill of his childhood, her one remaining garment fueled his imagination where its absence might have dulled it.

'Nene?'

She didn't answer. Carried on working.

'Nina,' he said, a little more loudly.

She glanced his way. 'Mm?'

'What say we go to bed?'

He might as well have slapped her. She froze for several seconds, the question hanging between them like a string of sudden icicles. He had an impulse to withdraw it, make light of it, but he didn't want to cancel it, he wanted her to say 'You bet!', and leap up, drag him inside, jump on him. What she actually did, after a heavy pause, was pull herself slowly up onto her haunches, chin down as though giving the proposal serious consideration. She didn't want to go to bed, he knew that. Nothing had been further from her mind. But he needed an answer. If it was no, he'd sulk a bit in the shade of his hat, try and forget he'd asked, and eventually fall into another doze; one that would solve everything and nothing. But if she said yes...

She got to her feet, slowly, pensively, like one about to perform some languid ritualistic dance. She turned away, stepped closer to the fence and gazed out from it, a standing figure against clear blue from where he sat. He might have called her away, not wanting to share her nakedness with any Tom or Dick reaching for binoculars down below, but he didn't dare disrupt the delicate process that might lead to her acquiescence. She never gave any indication of wanting sex these days – hadn't for years – but rarely refused if he asked for it. Took her time agreeing sometimes, though, as if trying to think up a reasonable excuse. If she was trying to think of one now she had an odd way of going about it, for quite suddenly she hooked her thumbs in the band of her briefs, tugged them down, stooped her way out of them, and, still facing the fence and the wide world beyond, waved them high over her head.

'Christ, Nina!'

She flung the flimsy garment skyward: a whirling aquamarine smudge against sheer blue. As her pants found a whisper of breeze and drifted across then below his sight, she turned and walked toward him in nothing but sandals. She stopped at his deckchair, frowning down at him as if to say, *Come on then, let's get it over with*. She towered over him, golden and glowing, brown all over except for the untanned region where today's briefs and others before them had been, highlighting, inches from his eyes, the bright tangle that he never tired of exploring. Standing like that, she seemed to be inviting his inspection as part of the task to be endured.

'Need a wash first,' she said.

He leant forward, encircled her legs with his arms. 'No, you don't.'

'My knees.'

'What's wrong with your knees?'

'Well look at them.'

He pulled back to do so. They were coated with earth.

86

He raised his eyes; surfed her crotch again, her brown belly, ribcage, breasts. She gazed down at him, her expression so blank that he suddenly felt grubby himself, but in mind and intention, and released her knees.

'Rude to point,' she said as he sat back.

'Uh?'

She glanced at his straining gusset, then walked round him, into the house. Will heaved himself out of the deckchair. Sharp twinge in the lower back. He stood a moment, massaging it. When he followed her inside he felt like a teenage boy off to the bathroom for a covert wank.

23

Early evening. Trying to force a loose fence post further into the hard ground at the edge of the yard, Will's gaze tripped down the slope of the hill. Everything beyond a good stone's throw was blurred to some degree without the glasses he wore only when he had to. Within the blur, far down, he saw a woman, tall, upright, standing on the path where it passed Slater's Spinney. Same woman as before, he decided, in approximately the same spot. Seconds on from that moment of recognition the post he was leaning on gave way, reeling him out into empty space like bait on a fishing line, clutching feverishly at unhelpful air. Just in time, he managed to take charge of his flailing body and jerk it back when it was dying to hurtle over the edge, and down. His first thought was not relief that he'd saved himself, but how idiotic he must have looked, and he glanced over his shoulder, saw Nina retreating from the window, into shadow. He took a breath, took two, three, and resumed his task as though nothing had happened, worrying the fence post a few inches deeper, settling for the resultant wobble in the knowledge that he'd done all that he could without a mallet.

24

The only notable difference between Billy Rainey's view and Will Tench's was that Billy's lacked a distantly humming motorway with rows of metal and glass sliding along it one way or the other. Standing there, Billy pondered the events that had delivered him to this point in his life. The training for a war he would never participate in, his dad's death, the inherited tenancy of the house and the smallholding that came with it. He'd been lucky, he knew that. A slightly stiff leg that ached on damp days, when he couldn't help but limp a little, that was all. Nothing much to complain about. It had been his ticket home, after all.

He gazed at the roofs of the village below. Before the war, they'd sneered at him down there. Thought him peculiar with his hesitant manner, his book-reading, his furtive writing and all. Laughed at him. They weren't laughing now. The wound that had got Billy invalided out of the Army suggested that he'd been doing something dangerous at the time he acquired it. When questioned about his limp, and the mark over his left temple where he'd fallen, he looked away, which incited speculation, especially among men who had personal memories of the First War. 'Poor lad,' some of them said, 'rough time he's had, don't wanna talk about it.' Some even looked upon him as a hero of sorts, which should have made it his turn to laugh. But Billy didn't laugh. Alone at Bleakridge, without family or even his beloved Jess, he laughed very little these days.

25

It seemed that whichever way the road turned the sun was ahead of him, and too low to avoid, forcing him to keep his head down. It was barely more than a track really, the view to his left obscured by a bank of thistle and wild grass, the open country to the right hiccupping uneasily toward cardboard hills. The sky billowed out around his head, deep and blue, as if poised to drop on him at a moment's notice. Henny Penny.

When the sun dipped behind the bank he was so relieved that he left himself unprepared for its full-blooded return when he rounded the next twist, and searing white light leapt at him like a silent beast. While cowering before the excruciating brilliance, somewhere within it he had an impression of a figure sprawling on a grassy ridge. Screwing up his eyes he identified, or thought he identified, a young woman, skirts awry, head thrown back in an exaggerated pose as though waiting for him. And then there were others, and raucous shouts as male figures flew out of the sun and fell about the woman, tugging at her, pulling and shoving her this way and that. There was laughter too, and the girl's cries amid the whoops of lads on heat. What to do? Mind his own business, walk by, eyes averted, or...

A hearty bellow from one of the youths and a half scream from the girl decided him, without any actual decision being formed. An anonymous noise as he rushed forward, still half blinded, into the cavern of light, lashing out in all directions but one. Derisory male laughter followed by curses as the young men scattered, taking to the slopes with coarse oaths, and then it was just him and the light and the girl splayed before him. He must have stumbled then, for there was stony ground beneath his knees, and her hands reached for his head and her inner thighs rose about his ears, and then it was all taste and odor, earthy odor, and hair, and consolation, and he never wanted to move from there; but when he did, no time later, no time at all, he was face down on grass, alone, confused, with a blinding headache.

26

The sudden harsh squabble of rooks drew her attention to the spinney at the foot of the hill, the spinney where Will had gone half an hour ago. She imagined him sitting in the heart of that huddle of ancient trunks shaping bits of wire round chunks of wood into something that would interest people who claimed to see 'truth' in such lame constructions. Once, he would have redeemed himself with a wink and a 'Who said there's only one born every minute?'

Once. Not now.

It was a long time since he'd produced strong individual things for his own satisfaction, pieces shown to no one but her and the odd interested friend. Back then, visits to exhibitions of new or recent work had convinced him that his was as good as anything on show, and more distinctive and potent than most, and he set about approaching London dealers, initially with the cheerful certainty of the innocent, but soon thereafter with barely-suppressed anger as the photos and small samples he showed them were gazed at with tolerant smiles and references to Gaudier, Lipchitz, Arp, Moore, the usual crew – comparisons that irritated him, not least because his inspiration was taken from further back than any of them: to the Vinča artifacts excavated in Yugoslavia, the figurines of the Tisza and Macedonian Sitagroi cultures, the vessels and sculptures of the Sesklo of Thessaly, the Chalcolithic Cucuteni of Moldavia – obscure to all but archaeologists who specialized in the civilizations of Old Europe. He'd spent years examining such things, drawing them for commission or pleasure, and later, when working in stone, it had felt natural to attempt modern evocations of some of them without actually copying them. He'd never concealed or denied his sources, but on the few occasions he mentioned them to dealers it was immediately clear that he'd bounded beyond the range of their interest. He felt conspired against by the various kinds and degrees of dismissal: sly sidelong glances, lofty condescension, smooth words with no light in the speaker's eyes. Entering a Cork Street gallery that specialized in sculpture he found two elegant young women in trouser suits disporting themselves on a lime green chaise longue. Attempting levity, he said: 'Don't get up, ladies!', to which one of them replied: 'We weren't going to.' Still reclining, flipping through the photographs of the pieces he hoped to interest dealers in, the only one of the pair who seemed to have working vocal chords said: 'Can't sell things like this in England today, try Germany, New York' – in other words, anywhere but here.

Meeting similar responses wherever he showed examples of his work he became bitter, particularly when he saw younger artists taken up and promoted when their work was undeniably immature or ephemeral, or both. But it was the way things worked. A late-starting sculptor without contacts or recorded pedigree was looked upon by the art world cognoscenti as less likely to produce anything of real merit than the humblest student preparing for a degree show.

Not that you had to be young or new to produce work that he took against. He developed a particular intolerance for what he called 'Why-Bother-Art' and the critics who praised it. 'The easiest way to get noticed in this game,' he said to Nina once, 'is to produce something so banal, so effortless, so corny that no one would've spared it a glance before, and proclaim it "Art", capital A. Hang a used sanitary towel on a meat-hook, write "Ergonomics" on the floor, and those shallow twats buzz round like bees on a bender. Any idiot could produce shit like that.'

'You couldn't,' Nina said.

'Oh no?'

He went to the bedroom, cleared his half of the wardrobe of wire coat hangers, carted them out to the studio and returned an hour later with a plywood box he'd knocked together and spray-painted bright blue. Inside the box he'd placed a twisted maze of the hangers, sprayed yellow. 'The End of Eternity!' he cried, and threw the box on the floor with a mixture of triumph and disgust.

Nina was amused by that. 'Ah, but that's a one-off,' she

said. 'Even you couldn't be so shallow that you could produce more stuff as asinine as that.'

'Watch me,' he said, and in the weeks that followed constructed many more boxes of various sizes, brightly colored, filled with household accessories and materials, junk from rubbish tips and charity shops, aggrandizing each presentation with titles that suggested some deep philosophy but which had nothing whatever to do with the item in question. Managing to slip some of these into small group shows he was soon able to consolidate his opinion that many gallery owners and critics had the integrity and imagination of chipmunks.

And so it went on, and in the going on he became known for such offerings. Known and applauded – a fact that in private had them both shaking their heads in amazement. His name started to get about, his opinions to be sought, opinions made up on the spot, usually far removed from his real thoughts. Once he said to Nina: 'I'm worried. Today I heard myself talking about my latest batch and it seemed to make sense, even to me. You've got to slap me every now and then or I might start believing me, then where would we be?'

At first she'd tried to remind him of this, but before long resistance kicked in, then anger. How dare she tell him what was good and what wasn't? What would a fucking nurse know? And she'd retreated. And continued to retreat. Articles began to appear about him. She heard a radio arts program interviewer warble something about 'the integrity of Tench's vision', the kind of sycophancy that would once have made Will choke even if applied to the pieces he'd struggled with for so long – pieces now concealed by dustsheets and black polythene so as not to affront the occasional post-sanity admirer on a visit. From time to time she saw something in his eyes when he glanced at her from one of his absurd creations, a look of bewilderment, as if to say 'How the hell did I get here?', but then, with something equivalent to a click of the fingers, the vulnerability was gone and he was again involved in his personal contribution to the planet's junk pile and promoting the hey-look-at-me image born, once upon a time, of a sneer.

27

'You've stopped shaving,' she said one day.

'I've only shaved twice since we got here,' he replied.

'Well, a beard would be a bit of a disguise.'

'Disguise?'

'If you think you need one.'

'Would you mind?'

'Mind what?'

'Me with a beard.'

She shrugged. 'Your face.'

'I had one when we first met.'

'Most of the lads on that site did. Few of them bothered to shave, ever.'

'It's a wonder you could tell us apart.'

'I couldn't. What was your name again?'

'I remember you saying that you liked my beard.'

'I probably did. It suited you.'

'Better than not having one?'

'No question.'

'You should've said, I'd have kept it.'

'You never asked.'

Perhaps the most intimate conversation they'd had since coming here, this was followed by an hour in which nothing was said by either of them. Later, he was sitting at the window doodling, miles and years away in his mind, when Nina – working on a puzzle in the crossword book she'd bought shortly after their arrival to 'stop my brain seizing up' – said, 'Will. That place we went to near Paris that time.'

'What place?'

'You know, the one where Vinnie popped his clogs, what was it called?'

'That's amazing,' he said.

'What is?'

'I was just thinking of it. What sort of crossword sets clues like that?'

'A cultural one. The name?'

He told her, and while she filled in the answer his thoughts returned to the day they went there, reliving it while drawing something that bore no relation to it whatever.

The popular history of the place, and the man, while including a degree of speculation, was well known. In the seventy days he'd been there he'd produced more than eighty paintings. He considered most of them good enough but often, of late, he'd found that while putting the finishing touches to a canvas, he could barely remember having worked on it, his mind having been elsewhere. Each morning he would go out early and set up his easel, pick up his brushes and in minutes drift away, coming back after a while to a finished picture that he found neither better nor worse than if he'd been fully aware of making it. Sometimes a rush of guilt at his lack of involvement would provoke him into at once beginning a fresh canvas and making a point of concentrating on its production. At such times his approach became almost vicious, churning and grinding the paint, forcing his will with pigment on canvas. There was a temptation at the conclusion of such rapid assaults to dispose of the results, but he never did. Their destruction would render the act of their creation – however unnatural – pointless; and besides, each one had cost money, his brother's money, which, as a married man with a young baby, he could ill-afford to fritter away.

On the morning of the 27th of July he borrowed a revolver – a rusty old thing – to scare off the swooping crows that distracted him while he painted. At one point he aimed the gun at the sky to do just that. Nothing happened. Annoyed, he looked at it. Fiddled with the trigger. Waggled it. The loud report startled the crows. They flurried away.

It was August, another August, a mostly sweltering one. On their last day but one they caught a train to the village some twenty kilometers northwest of the city. On arrival, they found the auberge with ease, facing the main square across from the town hall. There were no other customers. Nina, by way of barely-recalled schoolroom French, ordered a white wine and a beer, plus saucisson sandwiches because they had no idea what saucisson was. The beer was cold, the wine reasonable, the sandwiches revolting. Paying the bill they made halting enquiries regarding the man who had died there. The patronne beamed, pointed to the ceiling and encouraged them to go upstairs. Climbing seventeen well-worn steps to the top landing, where a door stood back as if the tenant had stepped out just a minute earlier, they entered a tiny attic room. A recessed skylight dominated the sloping gray ceiling. The floorboards were bare, the powder blue walls mottled and patchy. A big studio easel stood before a built-in cupboard. The narrow single bed – an ancient iron-framed construction with rusty springs – hosted a striped horsehair mattress. At the foot of the bed, a rickety kitchen chair whose rush seating was so torn as to be unusable; beyond the chair, a marble-topped chest of drawers. An ancient oil-lamp and a stone gin bottle had been placed on the marble. Nina walked slowly round the room, touching everything as though to establish and preserve its various parts and details in her memory. Will sat down on the bed. The springs squealed under him. He looked up. Through the skylight he saw crows wheeling and diving. Nina shuddered when she saw them.

Afterwards they went in search of the former tenant's grave.

28

Working the hill, daily, as his father had, Billy toiled long and hard that season, but however much he put into his labors the crops failed more than they flourished. It was as if the land was set on providing just enough for those obliged to live off it – currently just him. Often, on the hill, the days were very bleak; the nights, indoors, bleaker still. Whoever named the house, way back when, Billy thought, they named it well. For him, now, it was a place without character, merit or warmth. Where once there'd been the voices of family, now there was only his, when he talked to himself or shouted back at the storms that raged about the place some nights. That was the worst of it, the alone-ness. Not loneliness really, not quite. Alone-ness.

It wouldn't have been so bad if Jess had still been there. Jess was his constant companion before the war. After Mama died, he was all there'd been to love about being at Bleakridge. He couldn't take a dog to the valley where he was sent for training, though, and when he returned with his limp and his scar Jess was no longer there. With his dad gone too, Billy could only enquire down in the village if anyone had seen him; but all that anyone there could offer was a shrug and a 'Died or run off,' or, the thought of one man, 'Went looking for you maybe, lad, couldn't find you, or his way back.' Few days passed without Billy scouring the landscape for Jess, calling his name. A couple of times he thought he heard an answering bark, but no dog appeared in the bark's wake.

He might or might not have been looking for Jess the morning he noticed Ella Raines on the track by Slater's Spinney. Just standing there, she was, just standing. Her features were indiscernible from far up the slope, but there was no mistaking that hair. No one else had hair like Ella Raines. Billy grunted, very much the way his father used to at the least provocation, and carried on with his work. *Other things to do than look at females.* But after that day he saw her more frequently, down by the spinney or on some part of the hill, and before long he was disappointed when she wasn't anywhere to be seen. Still, though, when he did see her, he kept his distance. Still didn't acknowledge her, give any indication that he was more than a little aware of her.

29

Mid-morning. He was sketching at the main window when she came out of the kitchen carrying one of the mugs from the dresser. 'Coffee?' he asked.

'Tea.'

'Oh.'

'Did you want one?'

'Wouldn't mind a coffee.'

'Well, kettle's not long boiled.'

She seated herself in what had become her usual chair, in front of the black grate where a fire had burned last night. She had a book to hand. He considered asking about it, but instead said: 'I fancy a walk. Do you?'

She frowned across at him. 'If you mean round the yard, no thanks, done that, thrill's worn off.'

'Down there. There's a bit of river just beyond the spinney. Pleasant, day like this.'

'And to get to this bit of river you have to go through the rooks, do you?'

'They won't bother us.'

'They'll be watching.'

'The river's well away from where they nest.'

She said nothing more and he let it go, but after lunch she went to the door, and said, 'You coming?'

He looked up. She was wearing a skirt. A loose, light skirt that he could swear he'd never seen before.

'Coming?' he asked.

'You said you wanted to show me that bit of river.'

'Oh. Yes. Right.'

He jumped up. Grabbed his hat.

To reach the river they had to negotiate a downward path through disheveled woodland. The path being narrow and badly pitted, littered with shifting scree and tree scraps, they needed to concentrate on their descent. Nina took the lead here, Will following. At one point the sun, breaking through a breach in the dense foliage, bathed the arm he raised to lift a leafy overhang, consuming his entire forearm as if to neutralize its existence, a trick of a moment's light that startled him, then, when his arm reappeared, full-flesh, induced a laugh.

Nina paused; half turned. 'What?'

'My arm. It disappeared.'

'Uh?'

'Vanished clean away. So weird.'

'Oh,' she said, as though she understood, and continued walking.

'Imagine,' Will said, again following. 'I mean imagine if, in that instant, my arm really didn't exist. Suppose *I* didn't exist.'

'Working on it,' she said over her shoulder.

'I sometimes wonder if I do,' he said. 'I mean if I'm, I don't know... dreamed up.'

'Dreamed up?'

'Like a character in a novel. Not just me. You too.'

'Ooh, me too now,' Nina said.

'Well think about it. An English couple, a sculptor and a nurse, high-tailing it to the far north after a Mississippi church offers a million dollar reward for their lives.'

'Your life. I'm just the hapless tagger-along.'

'But it's the sort of stuff you couldn't make up, isn't it?'

'Unless you're a novelist, is that it?' she said.

'Right. Not a great one. A doddering old scribbler way past his best, living on a pension in the back of beyond, wondering what half-baked crap he can come up with next. I mean how real can all this be?'

'I ask myself that every morning when I open my eyes and find that in spite of the sweet dreams I'm still in the same shit-hole on that godforsaken hill.'

'Fictional shit-hole?' he suggested.

'Okay, so let's flip to the happy ending where we drive the hell away from here at speed, laughing.'

'He might not have that in mind for us,' Will said.

'Who?'

'Him. Our creator.'

'Creator?'

'The addle-brained geriatric banging out this crap in a crumbly old farmhouse in Norfolk surrounded by sheep.'

'Will,' Nina said.

'What?'

'Shut the fuck up.'

30

Just back from the river, sitting cross-legged in a well-shaded stand of trees picking away at some lines of verse, Billy heard someone approaching a little way off. Glancing up, sun in his eyes, he could just make out two figures, one of whom could only be Ella Raines. There was no mistaking someone else for Ella, the way she moved, held herself, that glorious head of hair, burnished by the sun.

Straining to make out more against the glare, Billy watched the two come to a halt on the grassy bank of the river. There, Ella slipped her sandals off and dipped one foot in the water, toes first. A pause, then she gathered her skirts, gathered them right up, and stepped down into the shallows, where she stood absolutely still, a golden-thighed vision Billy could have gazed upon forever.

He was still gazing, taking in every part of her that he could see or make out, when her companion kicked off his footwear and stepped down behind her. Settled his hands on her hips. Pressed himself against her.

31

She didn't move. Stood ankle-deep in the cool water, one cheek tilted to the smooth air, putting up with his hands all over her for a minute, before:

'This... "creator" of yours.'

'Creator?'

'Has he just written you a hard-on?'

Pressing against her from behind, he nuzzled the tilted cheek.

'No. Not him. You. You wrote this one. Just you.'

32

Ella – from where Billy sat a silhouette in the dazzling sun – remained quite still as the man slid his hands around her waist from behind and began inching them up, rib by rib, slyly, as though hoping she wouldn't notice. When the hands came to rest, time slowed. For Billy, the already quiet day fell utterly silent. There was no telling which way this would go. If he knew one thing about Ella Raines it was that she was rarely predictable. The stranger seemed to know this, for his next move was very tentative: a finger of each hand tracing a circular motion.

Billy wanted to kill him.

Ella leant back, resetting her feet in the shallows to ensure balance. The man's fingers continued to coax and flatter. He touched her neck with the tip of his tongue. Now one of his hands spidered down to her belly, and further, and dipped, remained there as they swung slowly together in the hammock of the valley.

Billy could have wept. It should have been him there, doing that. Him.

The sudden flurry of some small unseen creature fleeing

the reeds changed every mood, Ella's particularly. She pulled sharply away, stepped aside, returned to the bank, scooped up her sandals and walked off, all in the space of seconds. Her companion watched her go. He looked so pathetic standing there with the water creeping up his trouser legs, that daft hat of his crooked on his head, the bulge in his pants withering with his desire.

Billy no longer wanted to kill him.

33

Heavy rain for most of the night. In the morning the ground was soft. Squatting near the top of the hill, he scooped up a handful of mud and fashioned a small figure out of it, crude, over-endowed, a not-too-distant cousin of the Venus of Urbino, and as he worked he began to see how he might make some sense out of coming here, being here; how this unprepossessing hill might be populated with individuals of his own construction. Visualizing them, he decided where they might stand: a piece of flat, bare ground just below the fence. The figures coming to mind would look as if they were meant to be there; even, with luck, like they'd been there as long as people had lived in the vicinity. Before starting such things, he would need to make some sketches – charcoal on paper, he thought, dark, smudgy, heavy with character but not expression. Excited by this unfolding prospect, he took a breath, considered, and... no, he thought, I can't, I daren't. Such forms would freak Nina out even more than she was already.

But on the other hand...

On the other hand she'd loved his original stuff, been full

of praise for it, and the figures or near figures he had in mind weren't so very far removed from the pieces he used to make. Why not get some materials in, build a few small things, see if she takes to them?

Yes, what harm is there in that?

34

After parking the car and seizing a trolley, but before embarking on the unstimulating trek along and along the supermarket's parallel aisles, she stopped off at the magazine/newspapers/office-supplies section just inside and to the left of the entrance, and approached the display of new paperbacks. Ever keen on the chance discovery of previously unheard of but potentially worthwhile fiction, she picked up, one after the other, three novels whose titles caught her interest, each of which she replaced after reading the back-cover blurbs. There was one other that she was momentarily drawn to. The author's name meant nothing to her, but the cover illustration, of a large hourglass and a pair of old-fashioned round-framed spectacles, had some appeal. She reached for it, but then hesitated, decided that with such a title – *This Ruined Place* – it could be about her life as it was at present, and left it where it was, untouched.

Pushing the trolley round the supermarket, she took her time over the most undemanding choices. Anything to delay her return to that fucking hill. The elderly freezer at the house was too small to hold much, but with considered organization she would be able to get a fair amount in. As well as frozen foodstuffs and ready-meals, she selected items that did not need to be frozen but would still be edible days from now. She'd done little of their cooking even in Cambridge for the four or five years since Will enrolled in a Mediterranean cookery course, whereupon, enthused by the variety of a cuisine that purported to accommodate many cultures, he'd taken over the kitchen for such a duration that by the time he realized he was repeating his menus rather too often, Nina's interest in preparing even the simplest meal had diminished to a point that if he didn't make something they opened a tin or a packet.

A couple of years back, celebrating her birthday with Wendy, Don and Will at a well-reviewed new restaurant in Mill Road, Nina, eyeing the stylishly-presented dishes a young waiter had just served them, said: 'Shit waiting to happen.'

Three pairs of eyebrows had raised themselves at her.

'What?' she asked innocently.

'Shit waiting to happen?' said Don.

Self-mocking hands flew to her cheeks. 'I didn't think that out *loud*!'

Will sighed. 'You know you did.'

'Mm. Well.'

'Mm well what?'

'The world's full, these days, of wannabe celebrity chefs creating culinary masterpieces for their sophistiprat diners' delectation – '

'And ours,' said Don.

' – and all they do, their mouth-watering tours de force, is scramble down the noshers' gullets, tumble through their digestive systems, and the following day jump out, or get squeezed out, all the same, literally the same, as stinking gloop that's sent on its way with a hearty flush. I mean *really*, why bother?'

'Thanks for that image, Nene,' said Wendy.

Nina grabbed her fork – 'Any time!' – and tucked into her cordon bleu mushroom risotto.

In spite of such opinions, she'd eaten well enough until the flight from Cambridge, but at Bleakridge food was just one more thing that provided little pleasure, in company with the views, the days, the nights, the odd bout of sexual activity that she still felt obliged to participate in. With that side of things, the physical side, she went through the motions, the tediously familiar motions, knowing Will's preferences all too well, but it was a job sometimes to keep from telling him to go fuck himself instead of her. Pleasure of any kind seemed so tied to the past now, so much a part of what *was* rather than what *is*.

While steering the trolley slowly round the supermarket, distracting herself with products, packaging, sell-by dates, it came to her that whatever she might once have been she was now, quite often, not a very nice person. 'Nice', she thought: a word frowned upon by Miss Sutherland, her primary school English teacher, but... ah, what the hell. She was still nice enough to people she cared about – Wendy, of course; friends from work; all but the most unpleasant patients at the hospital; nice to strangers conversed with briefly in shops, behind counters and so on; but she knew she could be sharp-tongued, off-hand, pretty foul to others, Will particularly. In his case, this was far from new. Through all their years together there'd been frequent spats, furious rows, days of barely speaking, weeks even, at which times they hadn't liked one another one bit. As for love, well. What part had love to play in things? The wrinkled old adage about loving while not necessarily liking someone had always seemed a pretty loopy premise to her. She wasn't sure that she'd ever 'loved' Will, or anyone else for that matter. How do you quantify such a supposed feeling? There'd been a definite physical attraction between the two of them in the early years, and a meeting of minds over some things – films, music, aspects of archaeology, a great deal of modern if little 'contemporary' art. They'd also shared enjoyment of many TV dramas, sitcoms, things like that. Not often books, though. Fiction anyway. While she couldn't imagine not having a novel to read, Will had hardly picked up a novel of any kind since he came off his five year addiction to sci-fi around his thirty-first birthday. Nina had so often longed for someone to talk to about favorite authors and books, but that individual had never been him – another of the great unresolved negatives of their 'relationship'.

Unresolved negatives. They seemed to be accumulating. The distance that had so often been hinted at between them had become more evident with time as they found less and less to jointly enthuse about, culminating in the brittle silences that had become part of life at their present location. Silences that lingered tensely in those very few rooms; rooms that she, unlike Will, disliked more each day. Will's attachment to Bleakridge was a puzzle. All right, he'd known it as a boy, when according to him it was a virtual ruin, but that was then. The restored house was quite without charm, the hill it stood upon an ugly heap of mud, stone and weeds. What was there to like? In some ways the isolation was the worst of it. She liked to know that there were people within reach even if she couldn't see them. What she didn't like, didn't like at all, was to *imagine* people, as she had on several occasions here. Imagine or – by some quirk of light, sense or reality – glimpse previous or alternative residents, as might a character in one of Will's old sci-fi stories.

On top of that there was always, in the back of her mind, and sometimes very much to the fore, the sick event that had induced the wretched, brainless flight from Cambridge. Unlike Will, who since coming here had shown very little interest in the world outside, she was keen to know the current state of things, particularly with regard to themselves. On trips out she always bought at least one newspaper. So far, in these, she'd found only passing references to the threat on Will's life. What interested the papers more was that he had disappeared, a fact that had prompted some speculation that 'they' had got to him, though the general consensus among journalists seemed to be that he was in hiding with his 'beautiful flame-haired partner', which gave her a rare laugh. 'You should see me first thing!' Flame-haired was something of an exaggeration anyway, but she could live with that. Today, at the supermarket, she bought three papers including one red-top, and once she'd loaded the shopping into the car she returned, went to the café to glance through them over a machine-produced cappuccino.

There was news aplenty, as ever, but nothing pertaining to their situation apart from a small piece half way through The Times. She might have missed even that if it hadn't carried the old painting Will had made of himself that looked nothing like him today. 'Whereabouts of sculptor still unknown', whispered the subject line, which summed up the entire piece apart from the concluding paragraph:

'Since the arrest of the two fifteen year olds who admitted to breaking in to Tench's Cambridge home and killing his dog "for a laugh", there has been no word from The Church of God's Great Light in Mississippi that issued the so-called "American Fatwa". This isn't really surprisingly as the church's leader, Reverend Stoner, has been arraigned for incitement to cause bodily harm. There are unconfirmed reports that the church will be disbanded.'

Nina sat back in her chair. So Brancusi – poor, innocent,

lovely Brancusi – had been the victim of a pair of malevolent little shits for their warped idea of amusement. As if that wasn't enough to absorb in one sitting, there was also the suggestion that there was no longer a threat on Will's life. If the psycho reverend had been arrested, they could surely go home now, without fear of reprisal. But the news was too sudden, too immense, for her to feel anything much in a place where people came and went, sat and ate and chatted. Relief would come later, on the way home, and overtake her so totally that she would have to pull in at a lay-by and sit quite still for some time, staring at nothing, while attempting to regather her senses, recalibrate them.

35

A mere thicket or copse at one time, owned no doubt by someone named Slater, the spinney definitely qualified as a wood today, albeit a small one, the property, it seemed, of no one. No one who bothered with it anyway. He stepped out from the trees onto the track that ran alongside the spinney and gazed up the hill, and in the gazing remembered a day in the summer holidays when he was eleven or twelve, staying with his grandparents. He was standing right about here when he saw smoke, high up, then suggestions of fire. Some of the village lads, he guessed. Bleakridge was pretty derelict back then, and a good fire would almost certainly have finished it off had it not started to rain a minute later. Stepping back under the cover of the trees, he'd hoped the rain would be heavy enough, its downfall sufficiently prolonged, to douse the flames and save the house. The rain did continue, and vigorously, and the fire did sputter out, but he remained where he was for some time afterwards thinking that that old wreck of a place, the old dump he loved to visit in secret, could so easily have been razed to the ground just then. While thinking this, he heard his name.

'Will. Come along, Will. Teatime!'

He packed his musings away and, hands in pockets, ambled off along the track,.

'Better get a move on,' his grandfather said. 'Be in trouble if we don't. You know what the old girl's like about her perishing meals.'

All these years later he smiled. Gran and her perishing meals. He'd loved her cooking. So had Gramps, mostly. They were gone now, of course, Gran and Gramps. Both gone. Their very ordinary little cottage too.

36

Bringing the shopping in from the car, Nina tossed two of the newspapers onto the table. Not The Times, which she'd dumped in a bin on leaving the supermarket. Making no mention of the article that had lifted her spirits, she skirted its content in an attempt to get some idea of how Will might react if he knew about it.

'Will. That idiotic Christian fatwa.'

'What about it?'

'If it was called off, we would go home right away, wouldn't we?'

His response was not an emphatic 'You bet, like a shot!', but a hesitant 'No reason not to, I s'pose. I mean if it was absolutely *certain* there was no danger...'

'You sound less keen than might be expected,' she said.

'No, I'm keen, course I am, it's just...'

'Just?'

'Good to be away from all the usual. You know, the phone, the bills, busy streets, people...'

'I miss those things,' she said. 'All but the bills. Those things and more. I miss working. Being busy.'

'I like the quiet here,' he said.

'Okay, I'll shut up. Be quieter still then.'

She went outside, round the back of the house, where there were no windows, and set herself against the wall, the bland, blank wall, close to the tears that she would never let him see. She looked out, looked down, across. Fields, ridges, furrows, valleys, carefully-shaped woods, isolated buildings, the odd ruin, small villages, other hills. I'm on top of the world here, top of the world but very much not. Far from the top of my world. I'm powerless and useless. Vulnerable, pitiful, lonely. Yes, that most of all. Pathetically, foolishly, utterly lonely.

37

One afternoon, rounding an outcrop on one of the narrow paths that wound around the hill like unraveling rope, he was startled to find her right in front of him, while she seemed so unsurprised that she might have been waiting for him.

'Well, Billy Rainey, fancy bumping into you then.'

Billy flushed, muttered something incomprehensible, and hunched on by. Ella watched him go, just a little bit intrigued. Billy wasn't like the village lads. They didn't rush past her. Couldn't get enough of her, that lot, wolf-whistling, making suggestive remarks, pawing at her. Not Billy Rainey. Billy Rainey acted like he didn't have time for her. She'd seen him about a bit before the war, and more often since he came home from it with his injuries, but they'd never exchanged more than a few words. He wasn't silly or coarse like the others, though. Out for what he thought he might get with luck. That made him different. Made him interesting.

In the weeks that followed that meeting, Billy continued to resist her approaches when they passed, as they seemed to do more often now for some reason that he couldn't identify.

But then came the day she stopped before him, preventing him from going any further, and said, 'What is it you want, Billy Rainey?'

'W-want?' he said.

She took hold of his elbows and looked deep into his eyes. Eyes that looked set to panic.

'I mean what you got in that *mind* of yours, lad?'

He colored. 'Mind? I've got nothing in mind, I... I...'

He dried up.

She let go of his elbows and placed the palm of her right hand on the front of his trousers. He jumped back in shock. She stepped forward. Put her hand back.

'Nothing in mind?' she said.

This time he didn't move, but he was flummoxed, abashed, apologetic. 'I'm sorry. S-sorry. That doesn't mean anything.'

'Oh, but it does, it does,' she said, and she placed her left hand on his right hip to hold him steady, and began to fingertip and palm him through the coarse material. Billy didn't know how to respond. No girl had ever done this to him before, though he'd imagined it often enough, and now that Ella was doing it – Ella, the very best of them – he wanted her never to stop. He would have given anything for her to go further still, but Ella knew her man without knowing him at all, and she took her hand away, stepped back, smiling.

'What?' he said, as startled that she'd stopped as he'd

been when she started.

'Thought I ought to introduce myself proper, like,' she said, and turned about, and was gone.

38

Colin glared up the hill from the track by the spinney. He was pissed off. The house had been empty since last year, locked up, but there'd been ways to get in even without the key the Morleys left with Dad in case anyone expressed interest in the place. Couldn't get in now, though, not with people there. If not for them he could have carried on going there, gone any time he liked, strutted round the yard like it was his. Best place on earth when it was just him there, way above everyone else and the shit the world threw at him.

'You wait til I'm older!' he snarled.

Wait for what? He didn't know. But he'd show 'em. Oh, he'd show 'em all right. He'd show 'em.

39

Returning from the same town Nina had visited the day before, Will unloaded a quantity of materials that bewildered her.

'What's all this?'

'I'm getting the urge to make things again. Proper things.'

'Sculptures?'

'And some paintings if I've still got any in me. Long time since I've done any real painting.'

'There's enough here to last you for...' She shrugged.

'Oh, this is nothing,' he said. 'Lot more on the way.'

'On the way?'

'To be delivered.'

'Will, we haven't *moved* here. This isn't *permanent*.'

'No, but if no one wants to buy the place there's no rush, is there?'

'No *rush*? If nothing else, there's a limit to how much time I can take off work and keep my job.'

'So when we do go back join an agency. Agency nurses get paid more, you've said that often enough.'

'I don't want to work for an agency, always on different wards, with different people. I like it where I am. And I don't mean *here*.'

He smiled, not really listening. 'It'll work out. You'll see. Relax. Think of it as an extended holiday.'

'If I were taking an extended holiday,' she said, 'it would not, believe me, be in this shithole.'

He shrugged this off, too delighted with his new materials and ideas for what he might do with them to pay her feelings much mind.

40

Evening, the light outside beginning to fade. He sat at the table under the window, drawing, bottle of red to hand. He'd got through three glasses in less than an hour without really noticing. Again Nina hadn't wished to join him. Sitting in what had become her usual place by the fire, though the fire, nearly out, gave off very little heat, she was lost in thoughts of no real substance and failed to notice the jerk of Will's head as he caught a movement outside. He stared out, confused, taking the woman in the yard for Nina while knowing she was still with him in the room. A glance toward the fireplace to confirm this, and a quick adjustment before returning to the window, the woman, just standing there, not looking his way. Her not looking allowed him to study her, the shape of her, the hair as wild as Nina's used to be. But then he blinked and she was gone, just like that. He made a sound which to Nina's ears sounded much like a yelp. She frowned across at him.

'What?'

He glanced round.

'What?' she repeated.

He cleared his throat; shook his head. 'Nothing.'

'You made a noise.'

'Did I? Sorry.'

He gulped the last of the wine in his glass.

'I don't know why you bother with glasses,' Nina said.

'Glasses?' He looked at his specs on the table, not needed for close-up work.

'Take it straight from the bottle,' she said. 'Cut out the middle man.'

'What are you on about?'

She removed her feet from the opposite chair. 'Your business, not mine, but you and drink have never mixed well, and you're drinking more here.'

'It's what comes of not having a telly,' he said.

She went to the bathroom, closed the door, having no need to be there but a definite need to be alone. She stood briefly, touching nothing, before turning to the small, scarred mirror above the basin. She leant on the basin with both hands, staring at herself for the better or worse part of a minute, as if in silent communion with her mirror self. Stepping back at last, she found that she'd come to a decision. She left the bathroom and went to the kitchen for one of the small bottles of water she'd bought yesterday; then to the foot of the stairs, where she paused.

'Will...'

He had returned to his drawing. 'Yeh?'

'Will, I've had it.' Pause. 'I'm done here.'

He looked across at her. 'What does that mean?'

'I can't take it any more. I miss... my life.'

'Sorry, I don't...'

'I've had enough of this. I can't keep on here.'

He frowned. 'Keep on here?'

'Oh, Jesus *fuck*!' she growled. 'Look. Tell you what. Sleep on it. Sleep it off. By morning you might have got the idea.'

She stormed upstairs.

Will sat back and looked to where she'd been sitting a few minutes earlier, and from there to the dying fire, where his gaze remained for a long time.

41

He looked for her. Where was she? She should be here. But she wasn't, so he went on without her, followed a narrow back road between low thatched houses to a walled garden, where a young artist had set up his easel to paint the unattractive church at its center. The young man gave him a quick, almost guilty smile as he strolled by.

Beyond the church garden a path swung round and up, becoming a wide, climbing track between fields of golden wheat. The heat was intense. The sky vibrated. Nothing moved anywhere he looked. Rare echoes of activity in the barely audible bark of a car's exhaust somewhere, the mournful cry of a train whistle.

Half way up the hill he heard slow hoof beats, the crunch of iron-shod wheels. Turning to see a horse-drawn hearse accompanied by a dozen or so mourners, he got a move on. The tall iron gates of the cemetery stood open, a gray stone wall stretching in either direction, encircling everything within like the boundary wall of a medieval town. The air was utterly still in there. As still as the long tidy rows of graves. There were hundreds of them. Some were magnificent marble edifices with cheerful little gardens of flowering shrubs. Embedded in many of the monuments, grand and humble alike, were photographs of those buried beneath them. The photos generally showed smiling individuals in the prime of life, looking their best. Casting about for an impressive monument suggestive of posthumous fame, he investigated likely candidates. In each case he was disappointed: family attempts to prove esteem by virtue of size or price, nothing more. Time seemed to slow in the stillness as he set about inspecting each stone in turn, methodically following long avenues to their conclusion and returning by way of a parallel route. He made small bets with himself when approaching some particularly fine or untypical stone, but always lost. The sky ached above him. The sun was merciless. His shirt clung to his back. He wished he'd worn a hat.

Somewhere in all this, the funeral party passed through the gates. Continuing his search, he kept his distance while they removed the coffin from the hearse and carried it to a section of wall on the far side of the cemetery. He waited until the mourners had completed their business and withdrawn, heads dutifully bowed. Then, the horses' hooves again, the rhythm beyond the gate diminishing gradually until, in that dry tide of mostly old graves, he was alone once more apart from a solitary gravedigger thudding earth onto the newly lowered coffin. The sound echoed in the stillness.

It was some time before he came to the new grave under

the wall. The gravedigger had gone by then, his work done. At first there was no stone, but as he watched, a small gray slab rose from the earth just in front of the wall. Though the stone was new, he couldn't make out the inscription on it, yet he knew that this was the grave he'd been searching for. Firmly in place now, the stone began to age, collecting moss and lichen, and the mound of freshly-turned earth flattened and sank beneath dark greedy ivy which in no time covered it like a counterpane. Then, as he stood there, the ivy reached up, snared his ankles, tugged at him, and down he went, down and down, until the ivy had swallowed him, and he was stretched out full length beneath it. It was dark there, under the ivy. Cozy. Easy. Comforting. But then he heard a sound from somewhere above. He tugged the ivy from his face to protest at the disturbance, and saw her, fully dressed, lugging her suitcase across the room.

'Nene? What's going on? Where you taking that?'

'I'm taking it downstairs. Hopefully without falling on top of it.'

He sat up in bed. 'It's packed?'

'To the gills. Hence my struggle.'

'When did you do that?'

Reaching the narrow flight of stairs that began just outside the door, she let go of the case. 'I've been mostly packed for days, just waiting for the final shove.'

'Final shove?'

'The firming up of resolve. I awoke fully firmed two

136

hours ago.'

'I don't understand. You're...?'

'Leaving. Cutting loose. Getting the hell out of here. I'll take the car to the station. You can pick it up next time you feel like a three mile hike. Not sure where I'll leave the keys. Ticket office maybe, you'll have to ask.'

He threw back the duvet, stood beside the bed, naked but for his pants. 'You can't go just like that.'

'It's not "just like that". It's been building up since we got here. One more hour here and I'll throw myself off this sodding hill.'

'Are you just leaving here, this place, or...?'

'Or you too? I'm leaving you *at* this place. Draw your own conclusion.'

'But hold on, wait, let's talk about this.'

'There's nothing to say, Will. Nothing *needs* to be said, or it would have been at some point during the endless silences that have become so common here.'

'The silences have been endless because you haven't wanted to talk.'

'Okay, but do you ever wonder *why* I haven't wanted to talk?'

'Silence is something you do. Have always done. Not just here.'

'Yes. It is. Again, ever wondered why?'

'Beats me. Never could get inside your head.'

'Probably just as well sometimes.'

She gripped the suitcase handle and started down with difficulty. He reached for the T-shirt he'd worn yesterday, struggled into it, went to the head of the stairs, watched her ungainly descent, the case banging against her legs with every step.

'Where will you go?'

'Where do you think?' she said without looking round.

'You don't mean home?'

'Of course I mean home, it's where I live.'

'You'd go back there with that loony threat hanging over us? The thing we came here to escape?'

She put the case down on the last stair but one, turned to look up at him, but didn't answer at once. Tell him or not tell him? Shouldn't he know? Him of all people?

'Well?' he prompted.

The prompt solved it for her. 'The loony threat was to you, not us, and nothing's happened in all the time we've been here, so...'

'Nothing's happened because they don't know where I am. They could still be there, watching the house, waiting for me to return.'

'Well, I'm going anyway.'

'Have you forgotten what they did to Brancusi?'

At this she flared. 'I'll never forget that! Or forgive! Anyone comes to the door who looks even *vaguely* suspicious, they'd better watch out, that's all!'

They were just words, but she believed them as she

uttered them. She picked up the case once more and lugged it to the front door, where she left it while she went to the bathroom. He went downstairs and slotted his feet into his one pair of shoes, waited til she came out carrying the wash bag she'd crammed a few essentials into.

'Nina...' he said.

'Don't forget to pick up the car at some point before someone nicks the wheels,' she said.

'Nene...'

It was almost a wheedle, and it irritated her.

'Give my love to the rooks.'

She hoisted the case and did a lopsided penguin walk across the yard. Flinching at the morning's brilliance, he followed, in shoes, rumpled T-shirt, underpants.

'You might as well drive back,' he said.

'You'll need the car,' she answered without stopping. 'You'll be lost here without a car.'

'I don't expect to go far. Seen everything I need to.'

She dropped the case and waggled the key in the lock of the boot, tried to lift the lid, but it wouldn't budge. She waggled the key some more and he watched her. Since the central locking ceased to function about a year ago, all the locks had had to be opened manually, separately, and the boot's had always defeated Nina. Exasperated, he stepped forward, slapped the lid, yanked it up. When he reached for her suitcase, she elbowed him away.

'I can manage!'

He stepped back and she hoisted the case, hurled it inside. Slamming the boot she stalked round to the driver's door and got into the seat. She closed the door, struggled with the belt as usual, cursed it several times, finally managed to click it into place, turned the key in the ignition. After two false starts the car leapt to life. She ground it into first, lunged at the accelerator, and propelled the car out of the yard and onto the downward track without a side or backward glance.

A pause before he strolled to the fence to wait for the car to reappear round the side of the lower hill and plummet the rest of the way, spinning a fine skein of dust in its wake. Then it was hurtling along the track beside the spinney toward the twist at the end that would flick it through the village, and to the motorway beyond.

42

It began with complaints about chest pains. Then she started coughing. The cough got worse. And worse. By then she was breathing with difficulty. Long, slow, rasping breaths. Then she started shivering. Badly. Finally, three weeks after she took to her bed, Auntie Joan was gone.

She'd managed to put a little money aside, so Ella was able to pay the rent on the cottage, but it wouldn't last forever and the landlord wasn't one to let anyone live in his properties for nothing, which left her with a very uncertain future. She would soon need another place to live, which meant throwing in her lot with someone. But choice was limited, there being fewer young men in Pendersdell and thereabouts than there used to be, and of those that remained none had any real prospects. Ella dallied with a couple of them, but gave no serious thought to setting up home with either one.

But then Billy Rainey came home from the Army and found that he too was alone in the world. What Billy had wasn't much, but it was more than any of the others, so she set her sights on him, taking her time with the orchestrated chance meetings that culminated in that special introduction of hers, and finally brought her to the day she'd marked on the calendar to hook him for good and all. When he came down the hill that afternoon she stepped out from the spinney onto the track.

'So here we are again, Billy Rainey. Here we are again.'

Well, he went into his usual performance, coming over all big and oafish, twining his fingers, stammering an answer that was no answer at all, until she took him by the shoulders and hauled him into a more vertical stance.

'Say what you want to say,' she told him. 'Take your time now, don't gabble, I'm listening, right?'

And he said it. The last thing she might have expected in a casual conversation with such a shy young man.

'Marry me.'

'What?' she said. 'What you say?'

He said it again, and she roared with laughter.

'Marry you? Why would I do a daft thing like that?'

'Well, I... I thought...'

His shoulders slumped again, his head drooped, and he started past her, humiliated. She saw this, couldn't have missed it, and tried to make amends, in a modest sort of way.

'How old are you, Billy Rainey?' she said to his back.

He stopped. Half turned. 'I'm... uh...'

'Come on, spit it out.'

'Nineteen. Just.'

142

'Nineteen,' she said. 'Me too. Bit more than just, but still too young to be married.'

'Oh, I don't know,' said he.

'No need to get hitched anyway, you and me,' she added. 'I mean, look. Our names. Raines, Rainey, they're almost one anyway.'

He clearly wasn't consoled by this, so she went to him. Stood close.

'I'll not marry you,' she said, 'but listen, listen to me, the rent's due on me auntie's place and I can't pay it, so if you want me at yours...'

'Want you at mine?'

'You can collect my stuff, and there we are.'

'Collect your stuff?'

'You'll have to if you want me to move in with you, I got no transport.'

'Move in,' he repeated, adding cautiously in case his understanding failed him: 'You mean... with me?'

Ella chuckled. A real throaty Ella chuckle.

'Well, I don't mean with your *dog*, lad!'

'I don't have a dog,' said Billy. 'Did have, but he's gone.'

'Just as well, I don't like dogs.'

He frowned. 'Jess was a good dog. I used to go on walks with Jess.'

'You can go on walks with me if I'm with you,' Ella said. 'Walks and... more.'

'More?'

'Well, we'd be under the same roof, wouldn't we? Your roof. Sharing everything.'

'Sharing...?'

'Food. Water.' She paused. 'Bed.'

'B-bed?'

'Don't you want me in your bed, Billy Rainey?'

'Well I... I hadn't...'

'Thought of it? Course you have, boy. Specially after that last time, eh?'

'It's not a very wide bed,' he said, all in a rush. 'There were two once, two beds, but when I got home from the camp I found fleas in mine, so I burned it, and now I sleep in me dad's. The bed him and Mama used to sleep in.'

'No fleas in that one?' Ella asked.

'Oh no, I checked. But it's not a very wide bed.'

'So you said.' She gripped his elbows. 'Billy Rainey. You want me in your house or don't you?'

'Well certainly. I mean of course, if... if *you* want.'

'I'll live with you for as long as it pleases me,' she said, 'and you must agree to that or I'll not bother, is that understood?'

'Yes,' he said at once.

'Yes what?'

'I agree to what you said.'

'And no more talk of marrying,' Ella said. 'None. Right?'

'Right,' said Billy.

The following day he hitched his horse and drove his

cart down the hill and through the village to her late aunt's cottage. Together they loaded it with those possessions that Ella wanted to keep, hers and Auntie Joan's, some of which she hoped to sell, trinkets mostly, worth pennies, not fortunes. She took curtains and bed linen, towels and soaps, two rugs, a chest of drawers, a pair of chairs, but other things she left, having no use for them, and off they went with the cart piled high, blankets and ropes holding everything on. Up the hill they went, stopping once on the way when a chair fell off. Rather than struggle to put the chair back on, Billy set it beside the track, to return for later.

Before he'd gone to collect Ella and her things, he'd packed away his poems, which until then had been scattered all about. There were three hundred and sixty-two poems – some from before the war, others written during his training down south, several from since he'd come back – all of which he put in a small wooden chest that he called his Poetry Box. There was a cupboard under the stairs, and within this cupboard another, much smaller, barely visible in the dark down there. He put the Poetry Box in the cupboard within a cupboard, intending to take it out on the few occasions he expected to be alone from now on, add more perhaps, about Ella, beautiful Ella Raines, his wife-to-be in all but title.

43

He sat outside, just within the house's shadow, drawing with a felt tip; nothing specific, letting his hand wander wherever it wished, taking the pen along for the ride. Sitting there, sun beating down just beyond his personal region of shade, for a moment it was ten summers ago, and he was on a terrace with his back to the wall of the Tuscan apartment they'd rented for a week. Then, too, he'd sat in shadow, the villa being bathed in it even on good days until about four in the afternoon. Move out a few meters, close to the stick fence at the edge of the terrace, and on those days you were instantly sundrenched; but he rarely sat there, finding the green valley below the terrace tedious. While his first drawings at the villa had been of his surroundings they'd bored him even as he made them, and before long he had resorted to barely-aware doodling, and the doodles had become the figures he invariably came back to: naked colossi with thick-veined cocks and storm maidens with pendulous breasts, vulvas like clenched lips on the point of parting. Without planning it, these casual things became the starting point for a series of pen and ink drawings whose imagery had nothing to do with his surroundings; grossly distorted figures – male, female, hermaphrodite – whose lines were so fluid yet so sure that years later he could find little to fault in them. For him, those eighteen line drawings made the trip to Tuscany worthwhile.

For Nina, nothing made it worthwhile. Tuscany had been her idea. Her dream. It had taken her a year to save enough for them to get there and stay for a week, and she'd spent days flicking through brochures before booking an apartment in a villa thirty kilometers south-east of Florence. They drove there in the old Rover they had at the time, taking turns at the wheel from Calais through France to Strasbourg, along a spare rib of Germany, into Switzerland, then Italy where, in pursuit of the elusive road to Bologna he, driving, took a wrong turn and flung them into rush-hour Milan – terrifying experience for the uninitiated – before getting back on the road they wanted and continuing south. In a diary kept for the duration of the trip, he referred to their destination as the Villa Tortura, and to himself and Nina, almost always in the third person, as Fred and Ginger.

44

Overnight stop at a little place in Saverne. Could be worse. At 10:30 a.m., just before setting off, Ginger measures miles on the map with finger joints and announces that the journey should take no more than three and a half hours. They eventually bounce along the rutted dirt track to the Villa Tortura at the stroke of midnight, by which time tempers are somewhat frayed.

'Three and a half hours?' Fred sneers.

The Rover jerks to a halt before a dark building. Only one upper window of the building contains light. As Fred and Ginger get out of the car the lone light goes out.

'Fuck,' says Ginger.

'We'll just have to sleep in the car,' sighs Fred.

'Fuck,' says Ginger.

In the chilly early morning, after a very uncomfortable night, a figure emerges from the building. Fred opens the door of the car and falls out, complaining that his legs have stopped working. He gets up and approaches the stranger, a young German in leather shorts, who informs him that this is not the Villa Tortura but the Casa Fellatio. The Villa

Tortura can be found about 800 meters along the same rutted dirt track.

'Fuck,' says Ginger when this is relayed to her.

VILLA TORTURA, DAY ONE

Ginger writing postcards at a table on a terrace overhung with twittering foliage. Big terracotta tubs stuffed with geraniums and hydrangeas. Leading down to the outdoor pool, steep stone steps across which lizards dart like swift green tongues. Everyone else here appears to be German, guests and staff alike. The guests are mostly in their thirties or forties. They smile but seem wary of former enemies in their midst. Fred 'n' Ginger's apartment contains a lounge, a bedroom, a bathroom with a tiny sink. The kitchen is two dodgy gas burners lit by throwing a match and taking a dive before the explosion. No oven. The lounge looks out on the terrace. Three sets of French windows but no curtains. As Ginger is a great one for strolling around in her skin, Fred has gone to ask Herr Grenadine for some curtains as the occupants of the other apartments along the terrace continually march by glancing in every window and Fred isn't charitable enough to offer free perks to every Hans, Fritz and Willy goose-stepping through the Villa Tortura.

VILLA TORTURA, DAY TWO

Ginger writing more postcards, and a letter to someone. Tomorrow, she might write poetically about the *surrounding hills and olive groves, the vineyards and orange-roofed dwellings with their elaborate iron balconies bursting with bougainvillea. Today she'll write about the lack of sunshine, the gray sky, sporadic rain. Earlier she dispatched Fred to enquire about heating as there isn't any in the apt and she's feeling the cold. Herr Grenadine informed him that all heating is turned off at the end of April because the weather is so warm. 'But it's not warm,' Fred said. 'It will be,' Herr Grenadine assured him.*

Florence was a disappointment. They found it faded, drab, soulless. The river Arno was gray, the Ponte Vecchio sprawling across it less than grand. The Baptistery, impressive enough for its scale and the art on its walls and inner domes, failed to stir them. An immense cage of scaffolding enclosed Michelangelo's David, who stood in the street as if waiting for a bus to the nudist camp. When they separated for an hour at her suggestion, he wandered desultorily by the Uffizi. Feeling that he should want to go in more than he did, he considered joining the queue of mainly Japanese tourists, but decided against it even as he moved to do so and went instead to a café in a side street. The food displayed behind glass looked better than it tasted and the toilet visited before leaving was disgusting. Joining up again at the end of the hour, they spent the afternoon plodding the dreary Firenzian streets in hope of stumbling across some uplifting sight, sound, sensation. A few things worked for her but hardly any for him. The roads bustled and honked, crowds elbowed them off pavements, and he couldn't wait to get out of the place. For him, the best of Florence was the number of haughty women in black leggings and Renaissance-style jerkins.

VILLA TORTURA, DAY THREE

Rained in the night. Rained over breakfast. Rained all morning. Fred sits at the table on the terrace, shivering under the eaves. Ginger stays indoors, reading, mutters 'Fuck' a lot, for no identifiable reason. When they first met she rarely swore. Now doesn't seem to have an off switch.

VILLA TORTURA, DAY FOUR

Will the weather never improve? This morning Herr Grenadine strolled by, waved a hand at a patch of blue in the gray sky. 'It's going to change!' He made it sound like a command. 'I don't believe you!' Fred shouted after him.

Ginger not at her most talkative, so Fred keeps quiet too, but after a while hands her a note. 'Why don't we go to Siena?'

In Siena, dodging showers, they made their way through the overcast town via back streets and cobbled alleys. In spite of the weather Siena was at once more alluring and architecturally appealing than Florence. Her violent past seemed incongruous when contemplated below her warm brown walls, her satisfyingly irregular skyline of turrets and towers, palaces and pinnacles. Sky still heavy with cloud as they dawdled along a narrow sloping sidestreet. Nina went into a little shoe shop and Will, continuing on alone, stepped out into the vast, fan-shaped arena of the Piazza del Campo. And the sun came out. He drifted to the middle of the square and simply stood, turning his head around, momentarily happy. While full of people in slow-moving duos and small groups, children darting after flapping pigeons, he could almost feel the beat of ancient drums. In a month, a little less, the second of the biannual Palios would be run around the periphery of the Campo, but he wasn't sorry they wouldn't be there to see it. Imagination was sometimes more vivid than spectacle.

When Nina strolled into the piazza she stopped a little way from him and leant on her rolled umbrella to gaze about her. Minutes later they were sitting at a table in one of the unroofed cafés that spilled out into the Campo when another squall emptied the square in a trice. Nina was among those who fled, but Will stayed put, opening the umbrella and getting on with his hot chocolate and cake. Finishing his snack, rain still heavy, he joined Nina under a canopy. She immediately dodged away to shelter under another. A message if ever there was one. An elderly German couple motioned him to a spare chair at their table. 'Please, sir, sit down.' Deeply tanned, they told him that they were on their way home from Turkey, taking their time, enjoying various overnight stops. Of Siena they said, 'We were here last year at this time and it was worse. The Campo was flooded.'

VILLA TORTURA, DAY FIVE

Overcast start again. Intermittent rain. The apt continues chilly and damp. Ginger kicks herself for believing the brochures and neglecting to pack warm clothing. Late morning they drive to the nearest town, Castelfranco di Sopra, to cash travelers checks at the banco in the main piazza and buy bottled water and fresh bread. Fresh Italian bread isn't much different to stale Italian bread, Fred thinks, but they tell you it's fresh so you grin like the idiot tourist you are and try to shake the suspicion that they keep the best stuff under the counter, for their own.

The guidebook says that Castelfranco di Sopra was a Florentine military town. There's a military air about it still, almost of occupation. Easy to imagine hostile tanks rolling through the great arch into the piazza. Just inside the square there's a café. A photograph, taken sometime between the world wars, shows a bunch of old men disporting themselves outside. It had no name then, but today, according to the sign above the door, it's The Jolly Caffe. Old men sit there still, in the same positions, with the same scowls. Today's generation of old men. Not sure where the Jolly comes in.

In Castelfranco di Sopra there are two particularly striking faces. One belongs to a man who runs a supermarket in the square, the other to an official in the bank. The pincenez'd banker has stepped straight out of a Giotto fresco. The grocer is pure Buonarroti. Misplaced in the here and now, these two should be in different professions. The banker's quick smooth face belongs to an international art dealer or publisher; the grocer with his magnificent Roman nose and full gray beard should be a neo-constructivist sculptor in self-imposed exile in New York or Berlin.

Back at the villa now. Two days to go. F and G won't be sorry to leave.

45

Putting the villa behind them without regret, they'd headed north, through Emilia-Romagna and most of Lombardy until, some fifteen minutes after desultory conversation had flared into incendiary argument about incidentals, they came to the town of Bellagio, and were stunned into silence by its unexpected beauty and grace. Stopping the car beside Lake Como, Will went into the nearest hotel, the Metropole, and found that they not only had a vacant room but that it wasn't nearly as expensive as its location suggested. Nina – suddenly calmer than she'd been for hours if not days – told him to go and park the car while she unpacked. Spotting a couple of unoccupied spaces near the ferry terminal, he approached an official-looking man with a bag on his chest who'd watched him pull in to one of them.

'Do you speak English?'

'Aye, mate, like a native.' The bag on his chest held either binoculars or his sandwiches. 'If you want to know if it's okay to park there,' the man added, 'I say go for it.'

They were joined almost at once by a very fit-looking white-haired American who also addressed the man with the bag on his chest, with a question similar to Will's.

'You could get a job doing this,' Will said to the bag man.

Will and the American chatted for a while by their parked cars. The American worked in London, had come over by plane, hired the car at Pisa airport. They met by chance several times during the evening and following morning, in the street, at neighboring tables at dinner and breakfast, three times checking that their vehicles were still intact, unmolested, unticketed.

As they had only spent part of their respective fortnights off work in and on the way to Tuscany, Will and Nina stayed several days in Bellagio, exploring with pleasure, not always together, the fascinating little streets that climbed steeply between tiny doorways. Bellagio was as used to the British as the Tuscan towns were used to – and seemed to prefer – the Germans. Signs in shop windows made it clear that the proprietors were happy to accept English currency, which Nina tested by buying some chunky pieces of jewelry with sterling and not being diddled.

Evening meals were usually taken on the terrace of the Metropole watching the ferries go back and forth across the wide still water, the sun dipping behind the mountains across the lake, their only annoyance that they hadn't stayed here last week instead of at that gloomy Tuscan villa. Nina was well-nigh serene, at perfect peace with the world about her and the world within, but while their new surroundings improved the mood and outlook of both of them, the main beneficiary, ultimately, was Will.

Having gone out one afternoon with the intention of sketching the odd architectural detail or artifact unique to the town, he found himself in a narrow lane which, half a dozen paces along, turned out to be a street of artists' studios and workshops. Idly curious as to what kind of art might be produced in a town like Bellagio, he sauntered past door after door, some open, some closed, many of which were framed with examples of the wares made by the individuals who worked within. Tourist art, every one: local views, doe-eyed children, the odd twee nude thrown in as if for a dare. There was only one other person in the street, toward the end of it, a man in his fifties perched on a canvas stool outside a doorway, reading a newspaper.

'Buon pomeriggio,' the man said as Will approached. Will responded in kind, as well as he could, and would have passed by had the man not said, in impeccable English: 'You don't look very impressed, signore.'

Surprised, he stopped. 'Impressed?'

The man flapped a hand back the way he'd come. 'With the work.'

'I... haven't really looked,' he said.

A smile at that. 'But it sells. Some of it sells very well.'

Will could see into part of the room beyond, and some of the things in it. He said: 'You're not a painter?'

The man scratched his chin. 'Stone suits me better.'

'Does sculpture sell here?'

'Not mine. But the space is cheap. You want to see?'

'I... no, I... well...'

If his eyes had picked out shapes that intrigued him, his hesitancy was that of one who rarely enters premises where items are for sale unless they contain things that he might want or need to buy.

The man got up – 'There's no charge for looking' – and led the way inside.

All about, in the gloom and dust, were figures carved out of stone, far from beautiful figures, quite ugly some of them, not one remotely touristy, or, it seemed, quite finished. Will smiled at what he saw, and clutched his drawing pad closer to him as though afraid it would give its contents away. The man noticed the gesture, nodded at the pad.

'Signore?'

'They're nothing. Doodles, sketches.'

'Of scenery?'

He shook his head. 'No.'

'What then?'

'You'll laugh,' Will said.

'I might,' the man replied.

He did not offer the sketch book but flipped through it until he found a particular page. Then he walked to one of the crude works in stone and stood beside it displaying one of the eighteen pen and ink drawings made at the Villa Tortura. The man peered at it, then at the sculpture Will stood beside, then back at the drawing.

'You've seen my work before?' the sculptor asked.

'No. Never. First time.'

'But...'

The 'but' said it all. While there were clear differences between the drawing and the sculpture, they might almost have been made by the same hand. The sculptor's name was Georgio Raffo, and when he asked to see more of the pen and inks, Will showed him. Georgio laughed with delight when he saw them, for while none matched the first sculpture quite as profoundly, any one of them might have been an initial drawing for a work that he, Georgio, had carved or planned to carve out of stone. When he asked Will if he'd ever worked in stone, Will laughed too, and explained that he worked for a stonemason, as a laborer and gopher.

'If you don't work the stone yourself,' Georgio said, 'perhaps you should, because these are a sculptor's drawings.'

'Oh, I wouldn't know where to start,' Will replied.

'Here then. Let me show you...'

And he did, and Will stayed with him for over two hours, chipping away at a lump of stone with a selection of chisels, feeling the weight and texture of the material, beginning to see how he might release something interesting from it. With just two days to go before the end of their time in Bellagio, Will returned to Giorgio's workshop twice more, and each time was given further instruction and advice, and with each tap of this or that chisel he felt more at ease with the work and the material, a fact that Georgio readily acknowledged.

'You learn fast. You could be good at this once you identify your subject matter.'

He didn't manage to complete anything in the time, but as he was leaving the workshop on the last day Georgio presented him with a statuette, about fifteen centimeters tall, made months earlier but so like one of Will's drawings that he, Will, might have been its maker.

Will and Nina left the town with regret, taking the car ferry across the lake to Cadenabbia, on the far side passing Will's American friend and his wife strolling along the side of the road. From there they drove to Menaggio for the road connecting the last of Italy to Switzerland and beyond, and finally home, where Nina returned refreshed to the Central Middlesex and Will to Ted Slomis's yard, where, because Ted was such an amiable man, he made his first solo attempts to create something of his own out of stone.

46

At first it worked well enough. She was there all day, which pleased him, and in his bed all night, which pleased him even more. Even if she hadn't let him touch her, Ella's presence would have made him happier than he'd ever been, but she rarely refused his attentions. New to every facet of intimate physical relations, Billy had little idea of how to please her, or even what best to do, but Ella encouraged his curiosity and forgave his awkwardness as well as his inability to sustain his part in the proceedings for a duration that satisfied her. Oh, the things she showed him, taught him! Such wondrous things, during the performance of which he could ignore the scurrilous small voice whispering that she could only be skilled in them by having done them before, many times. Hating to think that others had touched her, been inside her, shared any part of what she now shared with him, on occasion he became melancholy, and sometimes, while doing his best to coax life out of the uncompromising hill with plough or hoe, he would pause in his work and howl with anguish that he was not her first by any manner of means. He kept his jealousy from her as well as he could, partly because he could not eradicate deeds and liaisons that had gone before, partly because, on the few occasions that he brought them up, she called him a silly boy or a fool and made him feel that he diminished himself by dwelling on such things.

Ella was not vain about her appearance. She had no reason to be. Nor was she shy in any way that he could tell. Some mornings, if she was up before him, he would lie in bed, half covered, hands behind his head, and watch her roam the room with little or nothing on, loving every aspect of her, every part and piece of her. Ella standing naked at the window was a silhouette that almost made him weep. There was no movement or gesture she made at such moments that he felt he could not watch forever: Ella stooping to pick up an item of clothing; stretching to straighten a picture; reaching down an item from the top of the wardrobe; sitting to brush her hair in the mirror of his mother's dressing table. All of these attitudes and gestures seemed to him unselfconscious, though they were far from that. Ella liked to feel his eyes on her. Reveled in the desire she stoked in him.

47

Alone in the house, this of all houses, first time in 25 years for more than three or four hours at a stretch. Nina wasn't merely out. She wasn't in the bathroom or kitchen or upstairs. There was no sound or sense of her. No need to tiptoe around her moods, her testiness, her belligerent silences. It was just him there, and once he'd got over the shock of her departure he found that it wasn't the worst sensation imaginable. Far from it. He felt... liberated.

To celebrate the solitude that he'd neither sought nor expected but found that he welcomed, he set about reorganizing the place to suit his requirements and no one else's, turning it from rented accommodation into place of work. He cleared the living room as well as he could, pushing the bulky armchairs against a wall, rolling back the patterned carpet, and set up a makeshift easel in the best of the light. Toward the end of the day he prepared a sufficient quantity of chicken and vegetable stew to carry him through three or four main meals, leaving it to simmer slowly while he settled down to bread and cheese and wine, which he followed with half a bottle of gin as a way of celebrating the great things he felt sure he would produce now that he was alone here. Stepping out for some evening air, at the front fence he viewed the perspectives of landscape at twilight. Its various planes, shaded hollows, modest eminences. Lights in a few windows down there, and in the distance slow-moving headlamps. No sound reached him. He stood there a while, but as he stood a wish for company came over him and he went inside for his jacket, then headed down the hill, intending to pop into the Duck and Whippet for a chat or laugh with Harry and anyone else who might be there.

At the foot of the hill, where the track approached the spinney, he found the For Sale sign lying on its side, as though pushed over. He left it there, but as he went on his way his eye caught something in the darkly clustered branches above his reach: the aquamarine briefs Nina had flung out from the hill the day he disrupted her gardening with the suggestion that they go to bed. He'd passed this way often since that day and not seen them there or anywhere else, so their presence surprised him. His thoughts, immediately scrolling back to that incident and the lovemaking that followed it, if lovemaking it was, were fractured by a sudden fluttering in the trees, and a rook leaping skyward. His gaze followed the rook as it pursued a spectacularly erratic course until, quite high up, it abruptly turned and took a dive, as if aiming at him, swerving back into the trees just as he adopted a semi-crouch, preparing to cover his head. Straightening up, he turned to the spinney, half expecting to see the bird there, but saw instead lips not beak, flesh not feathers, hair not wings. Flying hair.

As he recognized the girl she stepped back, deeper into the spinney, and darted behind a trunk. He simply stood, simply waited, until she stepped out, and back, and behind another tree. A further pause, and again she emerged, again stepped back, again hid herself, all the time watching him, as if daring him to play this game, follow her into the gathering darkness of a wood at dusk. And follow he did now, tree by tree, into the gloom, until she stopped a final time and he found himself on the edge of a small clearing with her at the center of it. Then she began to spin, slowly, arms raised as if to music. For a minute or more she span, and when she paused and faced him again she lowered her arms, held her hands out, took a step toward him. He did not move. She took another step, hands still extended, and another. Rooted to the spot – by her presence, her eyes, everything about her – a slow but terrible fear seized him, an unfathomable, unreasonable fear, and he backed into a tree, a shock that brought him to something like his senses. Groping behind him, he felt his way round the trunk, then put tree after tree between them, finally scuttling clear of the spinney and across the track rather than along it to the village. He began tearing his way up the hill, hand over hand, madly, as though chased. He slipped twice before reaching the small plateau that he'd earmarked for sculptures he might or might not produce. It being badly overgrown there with tangled weeds and wild grass, he stumbled, fell headlong, grunting as something harder than uncleared ground dug into his breastbone. He rolled off it, expecting to find a large stone or piece of rock.

It wasn't a stone.

It wasn't a piece of rock.

48

Earlier, Colin had heard his dad tell Mum that the woman had packed her bags, left the man alone up there. He didn't catch why and didn't ask, didn't care. Someone was there, still there, that's all that mattered. As long as one person was at the house he couldn't go there, couldn't get in, pretend it was his.

It was hard for him not to let his resentment show. Resentment, simmering anger. Until the new people came, he'd been able to get in any time he wanted. His dad was always having a go at him, usually for just existing, so Bleakridge had been his hideaway, his personal place. Up there, standing at the fence looking down on the village, he felt powerful, independent. Now, though, now he couldn't even visit. They'd spoilt everything, those two.

49

It might have lasted a minute, moments even, but, eyes still closed, the entire night seemed to have been filled with swooping flights over and through remnants of buildings whose occupants had long since fled or dwindled to dust, before the scene changed to others, at one instant a semi-derelict house in a wood, a man at the window, gazing out, then a house that might have been cobbled together by accountants or dentists, then a moderately imposing mansion gazing across a stretch of lily-covered water, then an insistent rapping sound, knuckles on wood, and a raised voice.

'Hello in there! Hello? Delivery!'

A jump-start of a wakening, in which he found that he lay on the bare floorboards. He sat up sharply, too sharply, but through the resultant dizziness saw that at some point he'd thrown up over his jacket and part of his shirt. At virtually the same instant he felt a pain in his chest and realized that the room was half full of black smoke.

'Hey! Hello! You all right?'

A face at the window beside the door.

He lurched to his feet, but before he could get to the door it was thrown back and he was blinded by brilliant light. Within the light, a man's silhouette. He reached for something to defend himself with, found nothing as the man stepped inside, stood a moment, then darted into the kitchen. Clatter of something heavy landing on the floor, then the man was back, coughing hard, almost retching, rushing to the door, where he stood gulping air. 'Like your food well-cooked, that it?' he said when he'd gulped a sufficient quantity.

'I made a stew,' Will said, holding his chest. 'Put it on the stove, must've dozed off.'

'On the floor?' He had no answer to that. 'I turned it off,' the man said. 'The stove.'

'Thanks. And you are...?'

A thumb over a shoulder to a brightly-colored van in the yard. On the side: LAUTREC ART REQUISITES.

'I forgot you were coming today.'

'Just as well I did or you might have been bolognesed and never known it. Where'd you want your stuff?'

'Oh... anywhere.'

He crossed to the main window and forced it open. None of the windows opened easily, and this was the worst. Outside, the delivery man unloaded a quantity of canvas boards and pre-stretched canvases, an assortment of drawing and painting equipment, armature wire, rolls of scrim. While he brought them in, Will dropped his jacket on the floor and went into the bathroom. He opened his shirt. A large purple bruise. He splashed cold water on his face, then went upstairs to change his shirt. As he came down the man asked if he wanted the tubs of premixed plaster inside too.

'No, stand them out there, would you? Against the wall.'

When this was done, the man came to the door again. 'Feeling better?' he said.

'Not much, but I'll live – unless the delivery's a front and you've come to kill me.'

The man handed him a delivery note and proffered a small screen. 'Put your squiggle here.' Will obliged. 'I would say have a nice day,' the man said, heading back to the van, 'but you look like standing up's the best you'll be able to do for most of it.'

'You could be right about that.' Will had followed him as far as the door. 'Thanks,' he added. 'For... you know.'

'Any time. Part of the service, saving lives.'

Slamming the van's rear doors, the man walked to the driver's side and climbed in. Then he did a four point turn, glanced at Will leaning in the doorway, laughed, and drove away, down the track.

50

Steven Dornick, 29, a Staff Sergeant at RAF Lakenheath, primarily a US air base since the late nineteen-forties, was an equipment accountability supervisor with the 48th Logistics Readiness Squadron. And he was something else too. He was bored as fuck. There had to be more to life than maintaining the wing's equipment program, watching aircraft take off and land, conversation with people who couldn't understand why he didn't want to talk about the same stuff they did. There sure wasn't much to write home about, even though Mom was glad of any news, however trivial and mundane.

Dornick first heard about the so-called American Fatwa the same time everyone else on base did, and the same way, through the TV news. At first he found the whole thing highly amusing. A Christian church offering money for the life of someone who'd offended it with something he'd made? What a hoot. He looked up the church's website and saw how heated its pastor and congregation had become about the work in question. The outrage expressed on the index page carried a link to another page on which Dornick found a parody of an old Western wanted poster. 'One million dollar reward for this man's life!' the poster screamed above a bad painting of the sculptor.

Dornick laughed again.

But as the story and the price on the guy's head achieved more prominence, his imagination kicked in. A million. Hardly a fortune these days, but a whole lot more than he had, and not bad for what would surely be no more than a few minutes' work. Minutes that if nothing else would relieve the tedium of life on base. He'd never killed anyone, but he spent more time at the Feltwell gun range seven miles away than almost anyone else, getting stuff out of his system, and he'd thought about it often enough: there were a number of individuals at Lakenheath that he would happily see the last of. But could he do it, even for a million bucks?

Before he could come to a one-way-or-the-other conclusion about this, two things happened. One was that the sculptor, Tench – and his girlfriend or whatever she was – had done a disappearing act. The other was that the Rev. Joe Stoner, Lead Pastor of The Church of God's Great Light, was hauled over the coals for inciting violence. So, all over before it had properly begun. Dornick felt quite disappointed about this. Wondering why, he realized that his pulse had quickened at the thought of eliminating the sculptor and collecting the payload. He spent several days in the doldrums before casually returning to The Church of God's Great Light website and finding that all mention of the rage caused by the sculpture had been removed, including the wanted poster.

However, spotting an email address for the pastor, Dornick, using a false name, sent a question: *'Has the bounty on Tench been junked or do you still want him taken out?'*

He received an answer five hours later. *'Why ask?'*

He replied with: *'I ask because I can do it.'*

And in return: *'If you're trying to trick me into committing a felony, God forgive you.'*

'No trick,' Dornick answered. *'I'm in England, close to the guy's home. He's run away but sure to be back. When he is I can make him disappear – if the offer stands.'*

An instant response this time. *'Offer stands. One mill, no questions asked. Now what?'*

'When and how would the money be paid?'

'Payment by wire transfer once the news hits. But if you're looking to trap me all correspondence with you from this address will be attributed to a Christ-hating troll who hacked into the church's account.'

'Okay, so how do I know you're not setting me up?'

'You don't. Sounds like we're sharing a boat.'

But after a couple more exchanges, Dornick decided to risk the correspondent being Reverend Stoner rather than some agent posing as him in order to nail would-be assassins. Even assuming it was him, there was a possibility that Stoner would renege on the deal once the deed was done, but if that happened Dornick promised himself that on his next trip Stateside he would do to the Rev. what he now intended to do to Tench, and let him know why before executing him.

So. How to go about eliminating Tench?

He would need a weapon, of course, but it couldn't be any kind that might be traced to the base, and from there to him, after they dug out the bullets. He knew a man in Brandon, just down the road – Lou Redner, formerly attached to some branch of the British security services – who claimed to be able to get his hands on a variety of non-traceable small arms. But before going to see Redner he needed to pay a visit to Cambridge.

Cambridge was about thirty miles from the base, a forty minute drive, and it wasn't hard to find the house on Alpha Road as it had been all over the news. Until he saw the place and its location Dornick had been thinking that something like a combat rifle with a laser pointer would suit his purposes, but standing in that street he realized how inappropriate such a weapon would be – no grassy knolls or other things to hide behind in Alpha Road – and scaled down his vision considerably. It was dark at the time of that initial visit, but there were no lights on in the house, the owners still being absent. It was a modest bay-windowed detached house with an unlocked side gate, so he was able to get round the back without difficulty. There, after a little poking around, he found a low window that could easily be raised from the outside.

Dornick went to Lou Redner to seek his recommendation. While not wanting to know precisely what he wanted a handgun for, Redner suggested a Brügger & Thomet VP-9 pistol, which he described as 'a smaller, lighter development of the Welrod 9mm Mark 1, built for British special forces during World War 2. Hard to credit,' he added, 'but when it first came on the market B&T described it as "a human dispatch pistol that won't disturb the neighbors".'

'They said that in the *ads*?' Dornick asked.

'Yep. Til they got a slap on the wrist from Advertising Standards or whatever. Then they took out the "human".' Redner chuckled. 'Took out the human!'

The VP-9 wasn't cheap, especially with the non-integral suppressor Redner recommended, but it was barely a nick in a million bucks. So he had the weapon and he knew how to get into the house. All he needed now was for his target to come home. With the danger believed to be over, Tench would obviously return at some point, but with no idea when that would be Dornick would have to make frequent sixty mile round trips and do a lot of hanging around in the dark in case he showed. For the drives, to cut the risk of being noticed, as he might have been in his usual auto, which had American plates, he acquired a cheap 2005 Nissan Micra, dark blue, which he kept off base, in a rented garage.

All set now, with everything in place, the routine began.

51

The smell of burning food lingered, but he got used to it while clearing the kitchen floor and wiping the cooker down. Attempting to recall how he'd made it back to the house the night before, the best he could manage was a jumble of abstract images and emotions that made no sense. There was something disturbing in this which, whenever he tried to focus on a fragment of it, brought a shutter rattling down, as if for his own psychological protection. So he turned his attention to the plan that had formulated in his mind before he downed that half bottle of gin: to go back to the beginning, or almost the beginning – square one and a half – of what he hesitated to call his 'art': drawing, splashing paint around, seeing what he could produce without overthinking anything. Fine in principle, but as the delivery man had surmised, functioning on any positive level was a challenge he couldn't begin to handle today. By mid-afternoon he felt sufficiently recovered, physically at least, to finish arranging his workspace, and by early evening everything was as much in place as it needed to be, but it was too late to start anything.

Next day he woke early and once the usual morning protocols were out of the way picked up a drawing pad and introduced charcoal to paper. Having deliberately given little thought to what form his first marks might take he was nevertheless disappointed with a batch of lines so inept that the page could only be torn off, screwed up, cast to the floor. He turned to the next page and started again, but when the second result proved no better than the first, he set the charcoal aside and sharpened some pencils – and his mind to some extent. Enough with the random approach! Focus, focus!

But, sharper mind or no, it was unable to conjure any image that his hand could readily interpret. There wasn't a thing that he felt the slightest wish or inclination to draw.

For the rest of that day and the one that followed, nothing but uninspired dabs and doodles tumbled from his hand. Eventually, giving up on efforts to produce something vaguely figurative, he attempted abstract accumulations of paint on canvas boards, and even these, in which anything could happen or be done, seemed ham-fisted and lacking in energy or point. He made several abstracts, each one no better than its predecessors, which, one after the other, he threw into the yard. In the late evening of the third day, he took the last of these to the fence and flung it out into the void, where a breeze caught it and whisked it away like a demoralized bat. Next morning, ashamed to have inflicted such a banality on the world, he went out to try and recover the thing. He scoured the hill, all round, but there was no sign of it. At the foot of the hill, where the track ran by Slater's Spinney, he also looked for those briefs of Nina's, last seen tangled in branches above his head. They too were gone.

52

The days yawned. Each evening he cursed his stupidity in imagining that now that he was alone, with all the materials he could possibly need, it would all come together, masterworks effortlessly evolve. Stuck for distractions from his failure, he clutched at domestic straws, going out to gather peat, logs and bracken for the fire, washing his clothes, cooking dreary little meals for one. Sometimes, mind elsewhere, he would lay two places at the table before realizing, and hastily scrap the second place. But even with her place removed, Nina would linger and he did not always shrug her away. For almost fifteen years she'd been his constant companion, most intimate confidante. She'd been there in all her moods and phases, through all of his, in good times and bad, through illness, grief, delight, first in Ealing, then Cambridge when she got the job at Addenbrooke's. He was so used to her being about that on occasion he would feel the air shift a little as she passed behind him, hear her in the kitchen or upstairs, and once, he went outside to say something to her and was surprised that she wasn't there. During one preoccupied moment in the yard she *was* there, however, walking on the lower hill, and he put his glasses on, and saw that the hair was fuller than it should be nowadays, and a little brighter, and that the way she moved wasn't quite right, and he blinked, and she was gone. But increasingly, now, he saw her – the one who so resembled a younger Nina – picking her way along this slope or that, sitting in apparent contemplation, standing on the path alongside the spinney. She tended to vanish suddenly, with nothing to disappear into or hide behind, but this no longer unsettled him. Another time, another place, he might have questioned his sanity or eyesight, but things were different at Bleakridge. They always had been.

Someone else who came and went without warning was the young man he'd come to think of as 'the farmer'. At first he'd merely been one more who was suddenly there, just walking or standing, but then he began circling the hill with a horse-drawn plough, or casting invisible handfuls of seed to the ground. Will never saw the girl and the farmer near one another, but they occasionally appeared at roughly the same time, and while she never glanced the farmer's way, every so often the farmer's eyes strayed hers, briefly, before he ceased to be, as if the sight of her, or recognition of her, ended his existence here.

The farmer's occasional appearances were almost incidental to Will. It was the girl who fascinated him, and before long he found her in his mind when she was absent, and took to looking for her. While disappointed not to see her, as the days passed she appeared more often, and then he would watch her, and have a sense that she was aware of him and not put out by his attention. It was the way she moved, and hesitated, half turned toward him but did not complete the turn, as though to tease him.

On the morning of the ninth day following Nina's departure he realized that the girl had become a substitute for her, a surrogate. Through all the years of his more serious endeavors, from his precise archaeological drawings to his extended painting period, to the stone sculptures following the trip to Italy, Nina had been there. She hadn't always been easy to live with. She was prone to black moods, wordless periods of gloom, screeching out-of-the-blue rages, but very often she'd been as tender as anyone could be, thoughtful, perceptive, capable in all sorts of ways that he was not. When he was sincere about his work she had never failed to encourage him, help him when he needed help, offer criticism that was useful more often than it was not. All of that had ceased when he got into what she dubbed his shit-for-brains-period, but even then she'd been at his side, at least during the making of the early pieces when, at his request, she'd composed accompanying tracts of distilled baloney of a kind that the world of galleries and art criticism seemed to deem necessary to justify the creations of its more outlandish fabricators. 'All you have to do,' she told Wendy, when asked how she could write such claptrap, 'is cross your eyes, think of Donald Duck's arsehole, and tap away until sanity returns and you go and lie down'. There was no shortage of material to consult for guidance: exhibition brochures' straight-faced appreciation of a bundle of wooden coat hangers arranged in a circle on a wall; a bath full of horse manure so odious that gas masks were provided for viewing at close quarters; 'the well-developed physical sense of the material characteristics of a cup and saucer balanced on an upturned bucket'; the length of red and yellow rope connecting the floor and ceiling of an exhibition space in which the reviewer claimed to have seen, in an 'ah-ha moment', 'an array of possibilities and interpretations'. Initially Will had looked upon these chuckleheaded ratifications of such artifices as keys to a bandwagon worth jumping on for a joke – a joke Nina had shared until the day he ceased to mock the praise that came for things he'd hitherto presented as vacuous dross, and started referring to them as 'works'. If this was when she began to withdraw from him, it took him a long time to notice, if he noticed at all.

But now, alone at Bleakridge, stuck for a way forward, he found himself wanting to tell Nina that there would be no more asinine constructions for the piss-brained suzerains of the art world. No further attempts to please anyone but himself – and her. Her above all. He had to speak to her, face to face. Convince her that from now on their life together would be as it was fourteen, ten, six years ago. Only with her at his side, spurring him on, would he be able to produce the kind and quality of work that he'd once been capable of. Work that few had cared for, seen anything in, and only one had truly loved.

Nina.

53

Some nights Staff Sergeant Dornick thought he would die of boredom. The repetition of the drives from the base to Cambridge, the long waits in that dull little street for a target that never showed, the weary drive back, it was all getting to him.

He was close to giving up for good when, one night, Tench's woman put in an appearance and let herself in the front door. He had no doubt it was her. The papers hadn't carried a picture of her but they'd described her as 'flame-haired', and this woman's hair was as close to that as it could be in the glow of the street lamp outside the house. The sight of her did wonders for Dornick's spirits. If she was there, the man couldn't be far behind.

He increased the regularity of his visits to Alpha Road.

54

The novelty had worn off, her patience worn thin. Bedtime was the worst. Billy liked to cuddle up and she didn't always want to be cuddled up to. Didn't always want his ham fingers all over her, his breath on her neck, his weight on top of her. It wasn't easy to hide her irritation, or her frustration, both of which grew exponentially. The one time she really let it all out was the day he came home from the market he visited every fortnight for essential materials and produce. Usually, needing to get out of the house and off the hill, she accompanied him on these excursions, enjoying the stir she caused among the men in town – to Billy's chagrin.

'Ella, please. Don't sit like that. Those men there, looking at you.'

She wanted to toss her hair and laugh and spread her legs further, draw her skirt taut across her thighs, but instead she scolded him for his mind, and he believed her, always believed her. But that day, that particular Saturday, the weather was gray, a little drizzly, and she hadn't fancied the long haul to town and back huddled under coats and waterproofs. If he'd had a car rather than a horse and cart she might have gone, but Billy couldn't afford a car, and besides he didn't see himself as a driver, so he said. He came home that day with all the requisites he'd gone for, plus three unexpected things. The first of these, shyly presented, was a bunch of yellow flowers in a blue earthenware jug. Ella loved flowers, and yellow, she'd told him once, was her favorite color, the color of the sun, of warmth, of hope. She had no difficulty expressing her delight at the gift of the flowers.

'I got something else too,' Billy said.

He went upstairs with a package that gave no clue as to its contents other than that they must be soft. Some minutes later he shouted to her – 'Don't peek!' – and she turned to the window while he came down. Then he said, 'All right, you can look now,' and she did, and she said, 'Well now, look at you, Billy Rainey!'

The suit he'd dressed himself in was gray with brown flecks, a bit too big for him, and he wore a tie, a yellow tie, 'To match those flowers,' he told her. 'What do you think of me then?' And he twirled about, arms in the air, as pleased as punch with himself. She laughed at his pleasure, and at him, for in that suit he looked the country clod trying to act the townie.

'Very smart,' she said. 'The tie, though. Bit long, is it?'

He lowered his arms. 'Mama showed me time and again how to knot a tie, but I always made a pig's teat of it.'

'Still, it's a good tie,' Ella said, 'and a fine suit. All you need now is some new boots.'

'Ah, well, yes, but I couldn't run to boots as well. Bad enough me buying a fancy outfit and nothing fancy for you.'

'You gave me flowers.'

'It's not new,' he said.

'What's not new?'

'The suit. Hand-me-down off the market. But the tie is, the tie's new.'

'And it looks it,' she said, 'and a very good tie it is, but what's it all for? We never go anyplace, don't have special occasions or nothing.'

He smiled a slow, shy smile. 'It's for when we get married.'

Ella frowned.

'It's my wedding suit,' he went on. 'For the day we walk down the aisle. Wedding suit, wedding tie.'

'I'm not getting married,' Ella said. 'I told you that right at the start. My rule, remember?'

'Yes, but that was before we settled in together. It's fine here, isn't it? It's good, you and me?'

She leaned toward him. 'My *rule*,' she said. 'I made it plain. No marrying nor talk of marrying. No *marrying*.'

'I know what you said,' he replied. 'I know what I agreed to. But I thought that maybe, now that we're all cozy here...'

'Well you thought wrong. Wrong, Billy, wrong.' She rapped his forehead with her knuckles. 'Get it through there, will you?'

And there he stood, downcast, hunched over, hair brushed flat from when he put on the second-hand suit and the tie upstairs. She saw this. Saw that she had to mollify him to some extent.

'Oh, Billy,' she said, 'oh, don't, I don't want to get married is all. To anyone. Some girls want to marry, but not me. We're fine as we are. We are, you know we are.'

'Yes. I do. But...'

She looked him up and down. 'This suit, though, my love...'

This surprised him. My love. She'd never said that before.

'You look so smart in it,' Ella said. 'I don't believe I ever saw anyone so smart.'

'No point to it, though,' he answered. 'It has no use, it's wasted.'

'Wasted? No, no. No. Special occasion outfit can't be wasted.'

'Can if there's no special occasion *for* it,' he said.

'Well, let's make one,' said Ella.

She took him by the hand and led him to the table. Stood him there while she hitched herself up onto the edge of it, skirts raised part way, knowing better than to show all at once. Billy loved her body. Adored it, worshipped it. So often he'd touched and stroked it with his thick fingers, as gently as he knew how. Always thankful, Billy. Hardly able to believe his luck, her being there, available to him at all times.

More often than she liked, though she rarely let on about that, seeing it as her side of the bargain. He provided for her; she gave him all that he craved and more than he'd ever dreamed of. All except marriage. That was the line she drew. It would take a very different man to persuade her into that. Someone who by his position or standing would raise her up from a life like this. Until such a man came along – if one ever did – she would pass the time with Billy, hoping not to get with child along the way. A brisk douche soon after each coupling mostly scotched the likelihood of that; or, where possible, the suggestion of a last-second withdrawal on the pretext, her pretext, of delighting in the resultant mess, praising the emission of so much as a sign of manliness, rather than a quantity to be endured.

Perched on the table before him, legs spread, she reached beneath her skirt and began to move her fingers. She wore nothing there, never did for most of each month, Billy knew that, and watching the rhythm of her concealed hand he was mesmerized, as she knew he would be.

'Come on,' she said, 'come on, boy.' He moved to take his jacket off. 'No, keep it on. Keep all of it on. Special occasion suit, yeah?'

'Not the occasion I want,' he replied.

'Next best thing,' she said. 'Come on now, get to it, lad.'

He began unbuttoning his trousers. The material was thick and heavy and one of the buttons was hard to shift. He bent to attend to it. Ella watched blankly, but when he released the button and hauled himself out and looked up, she enlivened her expression.

'Ooh, Billy,' she said in mock wonder, 'it must be Tuesday.'

He frowned. 'It's Saturday.'

'Even better, I love Sat'days.'

She took her hand from beneath her skirt and offered its fingers. He took them in his mouth and Ella giggled as if the pleasure was all hers, then shifted herself on the table, cleared the hindering part of her skirt, and leant back on her hands. For him, exposed as she was, as he was too, her posture was just right, so right that he knew that unless he could turn his mind to something else it would be over in seconds, for him. And then it was, just like that, before he'd even touched her, whereupon Ella's manufactured mood dissolved, at once, completely, dramatically.

'Well, that's good, isn't it? That's wonderful. Look at it, my nice skirt, my legs, all over me, everywhere!'

She shoved him back and flipped sideways off the table. Stumbled across the room, skirt held high to snatch a shirt of his that had been due for washing, and wiped herself dry, all the time venting her anger.

'You're useless, Billy Rainey. Can't hold it in for a minute, can you? Sight of me and whoosh, out it comes. Country clod, farmer boy, no use to any woman, no use to me, I tell you that for nothing.'

With this, fluffing up her soiled skirt as if to wave away

the essence, the smell, the fact of him, she strode out, leaving him to his shame, his misery.

55

Having previously checked the departure times with Harry Sewell, he walked to the station to catch the nine o'clock train – and missed it by two minutes. The next one for Cambridge wouldn't depart for very nearly three hours. He groaned. It being too much of a walk back to the village simply to pass the time, he spent the bulk of the wait sitting down and strolling around the station and up and down the platform wishing to hell he had something to read, a phone to play with, or... anything.

As it was, he almost missed the next train too, having nodded off in the waiting room. Fortunately a piercing whistle announced its imminent departure, and he scampered onto the platform and leapt aboard just in time. The doors closed and he threaded his way through the half-full carriage to an unoccupied table, at which he took the window seat. Another table across the aisle also had a single occupant, a woman of fifty or so, about to pour some tea from a thermos. As she was doing this the train started with a jolt, and scalding tea splashed her hand. She gave a small cry and glanced quickly about to see if anyone had heard her.

Will turned away and watched the station slip by, and behind them.

Soon there was a succession of signal boxes, concrete posts, wire fences, allotments with small wooden huts, a man heaving earth with a sluggish spade, a row of pebbledashed nineteen-fifties council houses, views into private rooms: a woman doing her face in a dressing table mirror, a couple in a bedroom preparing for who knows what: enthralling tableaux for the transient voyeur insulated by speed, anonymity.

It was warm in the carriage. Much too warm. Sun heating the window glass, turning scratches into wounds. The sliding view across the damaged window glass, the jog of the train after the walk to the station, the long wait...

'This seat taken?'

He shook himself, attempted to dispel any suggestion that he might have been on the point of dozing off, as if dozing in public were an antisocial act. He shook his head and the man reached up and dumped a bulging overnight bag on the rack and sank into the seat across from him, thrusting his legs out with relief as if they'd been curled up under him all morning.

'Party of schoolkids wreaking havoc back there,' the man said. 'Had all I can take.' A pause; then: 'Going far?'

Will glanced at him. 'Sorry?'

'Visiting an old chum in London, me. We were at school together, worked in the same office for a time too, til he moved to Devon. Kept in touch, sporadically.'

He nodded vaguely as if listening but then looked away, hoping the hint would be taken. When he joined the train he'd found a folded newspaper on his seat and tucked it down the side, out of the way. He tugged the paper out and made a show of perusing it. The headline didn't get through to him until the third or fourth scan.

HITLER ESCAPES EXPLOSION IN BEER CELLAR.

He stared at the bold lettering. Read it several times more before finding, under the DAILY EXPRESS banner, *Thursday, November 9, 1939. One Penny.*

A nineteen-thirties non-tabloid Daily Express? *What?*

He glanced about him, at the other two in this section, at the interior of the carriage. Any clues were so well hidden that for a moment, an alarming moment, he considered the possibility that this was indeed 1939 and that he'd imagined his life, dreamed it, read it somewhere. He looked out of the window. The fifties houses had been superseded by featureless fields, telegraph poles, the odd ramshackle barn, nothing that might be considered 'modern'. But then, screwing up his eyes to peer into the blue glare above all this, he saw the white contrail of a silent jet, and relaxed, madness postponed. He began turning the pages of the facsimile Express.

R.A.F. BAG TWO NAZI PLANES: Two RAF pilots of the Coastal Command patrolling over the North Sea yesterday won a fight with...

WARNING TO THE WEAK CHESTED! VENOS LIGHTNING COUGH CURE.

A drawing of a plump little girl with a hand to her mouth: *'Goody, goody... they're not rationing Ovaltine Rusks.'*

'Glorious day,' said the man sharing his table. 'Perfect for a train journey.'

German couple marry in London: a Jew and an Aryan girl, secret lovers in Berlin for years, were married in London yesterday – free at last from the fear of being seen together by S.S. men.

'But God, I could do with a smoke. That's the trouble these days. If you're a smoker you're made to feel like Jack the Ripper. You smoke?'

'Gave it up,' Will said.

'Me too. Five times in the past forty-eight hours.'

'As a doctor I am glad to see more and more "Craven A" smokers. Evidently people are discovering that throat smoothness and unvarying quality do make the world of difference.'

'The Restaurant Car is now open! The Restaurant Car is now open!'

A FOOD RELIEVES CONSTIPATION: Kellogg's ALL-BRAN, Sold at all Grocers, 7d.

'Wonder if you'd mind keeping an eye on me bag?' his fellow passenger asked. 'Like to pop along for a bite.' Will nodded. 'Unless you'd cared to join me...?'

'Not hungry. I'll mind your bag.'

While the man lurched away, he caught the eye of the tweedy woman. He returned to the repro Express.

'I had some very nasty sores on my hands and arms: after a few days the trouble began to spread. A friend, however, persuaded me to try Holloways Ointment, which I did, and after a few pots I am pleased to tell you I am free of every sore spot and the trouble is healed.'

The sun fanned across the window, forcing him to turn away.

The week war broke out Carroll Levis sailed home to Canada.

'It seemed like a miracle,' says Miss Rumsey of Acton. 'I actually looked younger in a week.'

In a few minutes he folded the paper and slid sideways. Standing up in the aisle, he banged a thigh on the edge of the table. Stifling a grunt of pain, he glanced up at the bag he'd promised to keep an eye on, decided it was safe enough between stations, and headed for the W.C. Just as he reached it the train plunged into a tunnel and everything went black. The tunnel howled. He scrabbled around for the door handle, gripped it, almost fell into the little compartment, with its grim yellow light and stench of urine. He slammed the door and bolted it. He unzipped, and the girl on the hill, Nina's younger double, conjured by no impulse that he could identify, filled his mind. She was smiling.

56

She'd been staying in Wendy's spare room since returning to Cambridge; had been back to Alpha Road just once, to collect a few essentials and a couple of small luxuries. Summoning the will to enter the house hadn't been easy, and she'd shuddered as she opened the front door, walked past it, eyes averted, murmuring, 'Oh Brancusi, my poor old fellow, poor old boy,' and leaving as soon as she possibly could.

While Wendy knew what had happened there, she hadn't seen it for herself and therefore had no such qualms; was pleased to have somewhere to go on her first planned night with a man she really liked. But getting ready for that night, she couldn't avoid doubting her own worth.

'You must think I'm a right old whore,' she said.

Nina shrugged. 'You're not so old.'

'Shouldn't I be past this sort of thing at...' She made a show of mumbling her age.

'Hope not,' Nina said. 'I've still got that ahead of me.'

'Yeah, but you and Will...'

'What about me and Will?'

'If not for that stupid fatwa thing you wouldn't have left

Cambridge and he wouldn't be up there and you back here.'

'He likes it there. He's in his element. Totally different element to me.'

'But he can come back any time now, can't he?'

'How d'you mean?'

'I mean now the danger's over.'

'He might not know. No radio, TV or other device that can be used to keep up with world events.'

'But people in the village...'

'They don't know who he is.'

'They might mention news items.'

'They might, and he might be staying there because he prefers it to here.'

'I can't believe that from what you've told me of the place.'

'Like I said, his element. I don't know why you're tarting yourself up so much if five minutes after you get there your hair's going to be a mess and that outfit'll be on the floor.'

Wendy looked appalled. 'Don't! We're not just going to dive into it.'

'Really? I bet he'll be expecting that very thing.'

'Oh, I'm sure he won't.'

'Don't kid yourself. He's a man, it's all they think about, whole bloody lot of 'em. What's his name again?'

'Oliver.'

'Oliver, not Ollie?'

'Oliver. He hates Ollie.'

'How very conservative.'

'His preference, that's all. He's got a good sense of humor. And he's keen. On me. Genuinely, I'm sure of that.'

Nina joined her in front of the mirror.

'Of course he's keen. Luscious dame recently uncoupled from a serial philanderer. Why wouldn't he be keen, especially with you looking like this?'

'Like this?' Wendy said. 'Like me? Now if I had *your* looks...'

'You do have my looks. Same nose, eyes, hair too now that you've grown yours longer. Why, we could almost be sisters.'

Wendy laughed. 'But seriously...'

'Seriously nothing. You're going out for an evening's physical jerking. A night's. When I see you in the morning I expect to find you thoroughly exhausted and extremely satisfied – assuming he's up to it, that is.'

'I'm not sure I am. I'm used to ten minutes max with Don.'

'Ten minutes? God, you've been spoilt. Listen, kid, you're gonna have a ball. Two balls. When we next cross eyes at one another I want to see the old sparkle back.'

Wendy sighed. 'The old sparkle. Yes...'

'When's Beck due in?' Nina asked.

'Later, not sure precisely when.'

'Does she know about your Oliver?'

'Not yet. No idea how she'll react.'

'What does she think you're doing tonight then?'

'All-night knees-up with old schoolchums. You won't say, will you? What I'm really doing.'

'Screwing your passing fancy's brains out?' Nina said. 'No, Mum's the word. What about David?'

'Don't tell him either. Him especially. Please?'

'I mean when's he expected home?'

'No idea, never sure with David, all-nighters are becoming a regular thing for him.'

'Well, he is nineteen.'

'Yeah, but I worry that he might be a chip off the old Don.'

'Worry another time. Right now, you have a mission. Now are you all neatly trimmed and powdered and ready to roll?'

'Fully coiffured, scented, reporting for duty,' Wendy said.

'Good, good. Now as you know the place is just how I left it the night we flew the coop and I didn't do anything when I went back that one time, but the sheets on the spare bed have never been used and should be vermin free, so do your worst on them – or best, as you wish – and you know how to work the fire in the front room if you want to use the floor. Don't worry about the fake sheepskin there, I can always have it dry-cleaned if there's any spillage – and it's anti-skid if things get a bit... you know.'

'Nina, *must* you fill my head with stuff like that?'

'It's not *your* head I'm trying to fill. Second-hand thrills are the best I can – '

A sharp ring of the doorbell. Wendy jumped back.

'It's him!' And with sudden panic: 'Nene. I'm not ready for this. I think you should go and put him off. Tell him I'm throwing up in the bathroom or something.'

'Wendy, you're more than ready. You're *over* ready.'

'As in over-ripe?'

'As in fully charged and ready to go.'

'Well... okay...'

'You'll introduce me, of course.'

'I'd rather not. Another time, if there is another.'

'All right, off you go then.' Nina held the door open for her. 'You look scrummy, by the way.'

Wendy's eyes widened in alarm. 'Scummy?'

'Scrrr*ummy*. If I was a bloke I'd have thrown you onto the rug already.'

'Rug or scrap heap?'

The bell again. Wendy left the room. Stood at the front door just along the hall looking back at her sister.

'Go *on*,' Nina hissed.

'Not with you watching.'

Nina backed away, theatrically, but then paused. 'Oh, Wen. One more thing. Word of advice.'

'Yes?'

'Don't be yourself.'

'Shove *off*!' Wendy hissed.

Nina closed the door between them, gave them a minute for quiet greetings and to leave before wandering through to the kitchen, where she gazed about her at the scrupulously-arranged photos of their parents and grandparents, hers and Wendy's, and Wendy and Don's kids at various stages, and framed sets of old train tickets, postcards and the like, reproductions of thirties theatre posters, the neat row of paperbacks on the shelf beside the tropical fish tank, the faintly tinted glass dome positioned above the circular dining table. She didn't display family pictures herself, and her sister's taste in décor wasn't hers, but she didn't dislike any of this. It was all so *Wendy*. Wendy's warm and gentle nature. It had never failed to surprise her how Wen had managed to so personalize their various homes with someone like Don such a prominent figure in them. She recalled her once saying that Don left the arrangement of their homes to her. In other words he didn't mind how they looked as long as he was at ease in them. Quite the opposite of Will who, in the early years at least, had sometimes minded too much how their places looked. Back then he liked to be part of the 'decision-making process' of putting a home together. That was until he was gnawed by the painting bug. Painting and sculpture. Once those sharp fangs took hold, little else seemed worthy of consideration to him. Fine with her. It had left her with a free hand to fashion their homes to her taste, which at first had felt like a boon, a release, but became less so, and less, and less, as he ceased to even notice her endeavors. His work had become all that mattered.

Now, of course, the freedom was total, though for how long she had no idea. It would depend on what he did next. She was relieved to be without him after so long in his company, but anxiety wasn't far away either. Anxiety about extended solitude. It was so long since she'd been truly alone that she wasn't sure how it worked any more. You're pathetic, she told herself. You should be doing what Wendy's doing tonight, with someone else, someone new, different, unpredictable. Is that what I want? She doubted it. She didn't feel a need to always be part of a 'couple'. Just being yourself, *with* yourself, doing whatever you want, when you want, consulting no one, just the ticket. Oh yes? Really? Could she face each day and night alone for a protracted period, perhaps for life? She wasn't sure. How odd that Wendy, in spite of her nervousness, viewed the vagaries of the future with quiet relish while she, being honest now, was a bit scared of it. Her present situation – sans Will – might be what she'd craved, cried out for almost, but anything beyond a small succession of todays was unsettling.

Threatening even.

57

Alighting from the train at Cambridge station, he found himself to be rather nervous. Nervous of seeing Nina. She was his sole reason for making the trip, but now that he was here he wasn't at all sure how to approach her, what to say to her. 'Look, Nene, I've reformed, no more crap assemblages for pats on the back by fuckwits. Just the stuff I want to do. For me. And you.' In other words, no more farting about even if the farting was more lucrative than non farting. But how would she react to that? How would she react to *anything* he said now? Should he phone to say he was on his way or just... turn up?

He'd been walking for some minutes in the general direction of home when he noticed the name of the street he was in. A street that had really gone downhill in recent years, in the process garnering a reputation for such felonious activities as drug dealing and prostitution. And he remembered the house number Wendy had included in the text she sent Nina after Don's departure. He remembered it because it was his own age. Number 39 turned out to be one of the tattiest houses. A peeling door with five buzzers and corresponding nameplates. One of the grubby nameplates was marked McWinnie/Mace. 'Mace' had clearly been scrawled in very recently. He held back for a moment. Do I really want to see Don right now? He stood there a further half minute, after which, as he still hadn't decided how to approach Nina, he pressed the buzzer. No immediate response, but then, somewhere within the grubby entrails of the house, someone flipped a switch. The sound of relayed silent spaces preceded the harsh, overloud 'Hello?'

'Don. It's Will.'

A surprised pause, followed by: 'Well fuck me.'

'Later. First, how do I get into this dump?'

A rasping buzz announced the release of the lock.

'Third floor, I'll leave the door ajar.'

Stepping inside he was greeted by a mingled odor of fish, vinegar and damp. Something else too, even less pleasant. The hallway was high, narrow, seedy. A dim light bulb cowering within a chipped plastic lampshade mournfully attempted to illuminate the antique-custard ceiling. He mounted the threadbare carpet of the staircase. He'd grown used to seeing Don in pleasant flats and houses made more than acceptable by Wendy's touch and flair. None of that here. It was possible that somewhere in this neglected building of many closed doors there lingered enclosures of chic delight, but he doubted it. He imagined myopic hawk-nosed tenants peeking through cracks in every door he passed, giving him the suspicious once-over. The half-open door on the third floor was no more inviting than any of its predecessors.

'Come in, young man, come in!'

The murky hallway beyond the entrance offered two choices. Through one doorway there was evidence of a recent fry-up (pans and plates piled unwashed on a rusty draining board), through the other an unmade divan and the corner of a second one.

'Where are you?' he called.

'In here.'

He went into the room with the beds. Don Mace sat on the second of them in a white T-shirt and blue boxers. One ankle rested on his other knee while he trimmed his toenails with a pair of nail clippers.

'Last I heard,' Don murmured, glancing up, 'you were pratting about in some palace up in Cumbria.'

'Northumberland.'

'Back now then, are you?'

'No, just... visiting.'

'Visiting?'

'Nina.'

'Way I heard it she walked out on you.'

'Drove out. It's not a separation.'

'What then?'

'She has a job, can't stay away forever. How'd you hear?'

'My house, yesterday. She was there, with Wendy.'

'You're allowed at the house?'

'Went to pick up some bits.'

'What did she say?' Will asked.

'Who? About what?'

'Nina. About anything.'

'Well, about you that you were still in Cumbria – '

'Northumberland.'

' – about me that I'm a cunt.'

'She called you that?'

'The very word.'

'Not one that Nina uses lightly.'

'No, it felt pretty heavy, the way she said it. Just walked up to me and said, very quietly, "Mace," she said, "you're a cunt".'

'And what did you say?'

'I agreed with her. Seemed wise. There was something in her eye, and it wasn't sleep or grit. And she did have a point.' Don took his clipped foot off his knee and slapped it on the carpet. 'I've fucked up, haven't I, mate?'

'Do you really need me to answer that?'

'Just checking the general opinion.'

'You've been fucking up and fucking around for as long as I've known you. Longer, probably.'

'Yeah. Nature of the beastie. But previous errors have been smoothed over after a while. Wen rants for a bit, slaps me around – metaphorically mostly, though once she struck me in the goolies with the telephone directory – then I buy her flowers, promise never to do it again, and we're back to watching Strictly Come Prancing, which I hate to the very core of my scrotum, and it's all hunky-wunky again.'

'Until the next time you fuck up.'

'Yes, and I have to work my arse off winning her back all over again. Bloody exhausting, I can tell you. This time, though, I have a feeling it might take her a wee bit longer than usual to get over it.'

'You really think she will?'

'Oh, she has to. I couldn't live without my Wen. We've known each other since our teens.'

'Yes, and wasn't it a teenager this time? A sixteen year old?'

'In my defense,' Don said, 'she looked older. Acted it too. You should've seen her. Unbelievable. I took pictures.' He reached for the phone beside him on the bed. 'Here.'

Will leant forward and pressed Don's hand, and the phone it held. Don looked at him in surprise.

'What?'

'Nina's right,' Will said. 'You are a cunt.'

Don sighed. 'I don't mean to be.'

'No, course you don't, it's a gift.'

'Curse more like. Can we change the subject?' He got to work on his other foot. 'Such as to why you've come all the way from Cum... wherever... to see Nina. What's going on with you two? It's not just her job, is it, not really?'

'She left in a bit of a huff, that's all.'

'Huffs,' Don said. 'They do them so well, those two, don't

they? Some sort of family trait maybe.'

Will tugged a kitchen chair from its place at the Formica-topped table in the center of the room. The chair wobbled under him when he sat on it.

'To avoid any tragic beating about the bush,' Don said, 'if the surprise visit is about you asking me for a loan you can forget it. I'm minto-skinto, up to me bleeding necko. Two homes don't come cheap, y'know, even when one of 'em's a pit like this. It's the kids. Gotta be fed, I hear. Lazy sods, they should be self-supporting by now, their age.'

'I was just passing,' Will said.

'Passing?'

'And I recognized your address.'

'I didn't know you knew it.'

'Wendy provided it in a text.'

'Ah, bless her.'

Don stretched out his foot to admire his workmanship. The gusset of his boxers jumped open and a testicle squeezed out. It popped itself back in when he stood up and padded across to the other bed, the unmade one. He knelt down beside it and hauled out a very scuffed brown suitcase. Throwing back the lid he rummaged inside until he found what he was looking for.

'And you're going back, are you?' he said, getting to his feet. 'Oop North. Staying there, on your lonesome?'

'For now. Maybe not for long. Depends.'

'On?'

'Dunno yet.'

Don strolled back toward his own bed with a large tin of talcum powder, lavishly powdering his armpits, then holding out the front of his boxers and shaking the can at their contents. He flipped the tin onto his bed and went to a narrow plywood wardrobe leaning against a wall. He took out a navy blue suit on a wire hanger.

'On your way out?' Will asked.

'In more ways than one, some would say. But yes. Mustn't let oneself get into a rut, old bean.'

'Not a night out with the lads, I assume.'

'I don't do nights out with lads, son, you should know that.'

'So...?'

'So you don't need to know.'

'In case I pass it around.'

'Preee-cisely.'

Don took a shirt and tie from the wardrobe, put the shirt on, slipped the tie inside the collar and began forming a knot in the small shaving mirror hanging on the outside of the wardrobe door.

'Hard to imagine you sharing,' Will said.

'Sharing what?'

'This place.'

'I shared with Wen and the kids.'

'Not quite the same thing.'

'Cheapest I could get at short notice,' Don said. 'And

you'd find it even harder to imagine if you knew the geezer.'

'Why, what's wrong with him?'

'You name it. Some people can charm the birds off the trees, they say. Not McWinnie. His is the kind of charm that puts the birds right back *on* the trees. He looks like a free gift from War on Want – works in a rubber factory, brake linings or some such – comes in every night smelling like a giant fucking McDurex.'

The knot completed to his satisfaction, Don stepped into his suit trousers. He had to give up breathing to close the zip.

'Which is why,' he concluded, 'you find me in such a tearing hurry to get out of here. He could be back any – '

A sudden rattling at the door suggested that someone was having difficulty with a key.

'Shit,' Don said. 'This is your fault. All this unscheduled chat.'

A crash as the door was thrown back against the wall, a second crash as it was thrown shut. An alarmingly bony man in his mid-fifties with close-cropped gray hair, a very long neck and a sour expression mooched in. He wore an old sports jacket over stained blue overalls and carried a canvas lunch bag. A look of intense suspicion settled on his face when he saw Will. 'Who's this?' he demanded in a clipped Glasgow accent.

'Meet Mr. Personality McWinnie,' Don said to Will. 'Duncan to his friend. I'm guessing that he might have had one once.'

'Huh!' Duncan said, stripping his jacket off. Without the jacket he somehow managed to look even more gaunt in the ill-fitting overalls.

He hung his jacket over a dressing gown on the back of the door, and, turning from the door, noticed the suitcase Don had pulled out from under the bed. His face darkened further.

'Mace. How many times have I told you to leave my things alone?'

Don shrugged. 'Sorry, lost count.'

He put his suit jacket on while his flatmate dropped to his knees to riffle through the contents of his suitcase. 'It's me talc, isn't it?' Duncan said. 'You been at my talc again. I warned you about that.' He rose, almost shaking with rage. 'Where is it, you thief? What have you done with my talc?'

Don strolled to his bed and picked up the tin of talcum powder. 'Would this be what you're after, my good man?'

'Why can't you buy your own, that's what I want to know. Why do you have to use mine all the time, that stuff comes expensive.'

'Precisely why I don't buy my own, me old sporran,' Don said. 'And if you don't want me to use it why leave it lying about?'

'It wasn't lying about, it was in me suitcase.'

'Oh, right, the next best thing to the Bank of Scotland.'

'Aye, well you've had your chance, pal. You've proved yet again that you can't be trusted. From now on I'm keeping me case locked, locked tight, see?'

'Locked with what?' Don said. 'You lost the key. You told me.'

'Yeah, well I found it.'

'Oh yes? Let's see it.'

'What?'

'The key. Show us the key.'

'No.'

'Why not if it exists?'

'Because I don't choose to.' Duncan gave an assertive downward jerk of the jaw as if to pronounce that the end of the matter.

'What a prick,' Don muttered.

'That's all you know,' said Duncan.

'Oh, I know more than that,' Don said. 'I also know that you're a prat. Now the thing is that some people are born prats and some become prats, but you, you're in a class of your own. You must have blue blood in those bits of string you call veins. Why? Because you're a royal prat. A right royal prick of a prat.'

'Do you hear the way he talks to me?' Duncan said to Will, whom he'd ignored since making his entrance.

'And even if you did have a key,' Don added, 'even if you did, so what? I mean, what's that case made of? Cardboard. Not exactly a crowbar job to get in there, is it? Spill a cup of warm tea over it and it'll fucking dissolve.'

Duncan affected an air of calm, chin slightly raised. 'Will

you give it back please? Me talc?' He asked this from half the room away, holding out a long-fingered hand.

'Come and get it,' Don said, weighing the tin in his palm.

'No, you borrowed it, you return it.'

Don laughed. 'Well if that's what you want. Catch!'

He tossed the tin not precisely in the direction of its owner. Duncan, unprepared, dived for it too late and instead of grasping the tin knocked it with an outstretched finger. The tin span off at a new tangent, striking the wall and rebounding to land within half a yard of Duncan, sprawling on the floor. The force of the impact flipped the lid off the tin and a fine white powder erupted like a small atomic explosion.

'I said catch it,' Don said, 'not do a Swan Lake with it.'

Duncan hauled himself to his knees, the fine powder dribbling down onto him. 'Me talc,' he muttered in a weak, almost tearful voice. 'Me best talc.'

He began scooping the powder into the tin with the palm of his hand. When he'd put a fair amount in, he got to his feet and drifted like a gaunt shadow from the room.

'Is it always like this here?' Will asked.

'You misunderstand, my friend,' Don said. 'This is one of the good days.'

'Is there a toilet I can use?'

'Yeah, go to the end of the street, there's a public one by the vandalized bus shelter.'

'You're joking.'

'Yes. Out on the landing. Second door on the right.'

'I haven't lived in a place like this since I was eighteen,' Will said.

'Bet you've missed it, haven't you?'

As Will approached the door, Duncan returned with a dustpan and brush and dropped to his knees to sweep up the residue of his talc.

58

The bathroom that served all the third floor tenants was large and stark, with its own delightful potpourri of odors. The old wooden seat of the lavatory, snapped in two in some bygone age, was held together by a metal brace screwed into the underside of its halves. The seat was already up, so he didn't have to touch it. Finishing, he zipped up and made three attempts to flush the toilet before succeeding. At the sink he turned on the hot tap, which spluttered reluctantly and issued cold water only, embellishing the brown trail formulated over the years. Someone had shaved over the basin recently. Scum on the surface of the shaving water had fled to the sides of the bowl when the water belched down the plughole, leaving a tangled necklace of dark hairs. Turning the tap off, he winced at the resultant squeal and raised his damp hands to his face to soothe away the weariness of the long train journey. Given the tone of the room and the building, he looked appropriately disreputable in the cracked mirror above the basin.

On the way back along the landing he very nearly collided with Duncan, backing out of the broom cupboard after returning the dustpan and brush. For a moment they stared at one another, as strangers blocking one another's way might, a moment in which Duncan, to Will, bore the vaguely puzzled air and demeanor of someone who might belong to any age but this; was bewildered to find himself in the here and now, yet unable to find any words that came close to expressing his sense of displacement. Will walked past him, back into the room, and Duncan followed just two paces behind.

'Thank Christ!' Don cried, tearing off his jacket, flinging it onto his bed, racing past them.

They heard the bathroom door slam, its rusty bolt hammer home. While Duncan went to the table, extracting a tobacco tin from a pocket of his overalls, Will seated himself on a corner of Don's bed to await his return.

'Ever think of doing yourself in?' Duncan said suddenly.

'Eh?'

'I do. All the time.'

He returned to the door and from a pocket of his sports jacket extracted something which, approaching Will, he held out for inspection. It was a pistol, old and battered, its handle severely dented as if it had been dropped from a great height.

'You can hold it if you like,' Duncan said.

Will shook his head. 'What are you doing with it?'

'I found it.'

'Found it where?'

'That's my business.'

'It isn't loaded, is it?'

'Course it's loaded. What's the point of a thing like this if it's not loaded?'

'It was in your jacket,' Will said. 'You take it to work with you? Take a loaded gun to work?'

'Aye.' He made it sound as natural as taking a flask and sandwiches.

'What for?'

'Because if I left it here, your mate'd've fished it out by now.'

'If he found that he might be more careful how he spoke to you,' Will said.

A canny expression etched itself into Duncan's sallow features. 'This is my secret. He's not to know about it. No one's to know.'

'So why show it to me?'

The look in the man's eye became one of unease, as if he'd only now realized the risk of sharing his secret with his enemy's friend. His neck became even longer, stretching veins and flesh to the limit, as he leaned down and stuck his face closer. His breath smelt like boiled cabbage.

'You won't tell him,' he said. 'You wouldn't, would you? Wouldn't tell him?'

'Not if you don't want me to, no.'

The gun, pointing nowhere in particular, sat between them, the butt of it in Duncan's hand.

'Swear you won't tell a soul,' Duncan whispered.

'Fine,' said Will.

Duncan scowled. 'Swear!'

'Jesus, yes, I swear I won't tell, now put that bloody thing away, will you?'

Duncan nodded, and straightened up, took a step back, let the gun drop the length of his arm.

'What do you keep it for anyway?' Will asked.

For a moment it seemed that Duncan wouldn't reply but then he raised his hand, slowly, and settled the barrel of the gun against his temple. His face took on a look of rumpled ecstasy. His voice dreamed.

'One second, that's all it'd take. No more piss-takers, no more working like fuck at the factory, no more shit like I get from your mate.' He smirked at a treasured image, eyes very bright. '*He'd* have to clear up the mess for a change. That'd be a laugh. Have to show me some respect then, wouldn't he? No more walking all over me like I'm a friggin' doormat, no sir. One second. Squeeze. Bang. All over.'

His arm had become tense, the barrel of the gun angled more acutely, his finger coiling more tightly round the trigger. Will watched. Waited. The slightest movement or sound might provoke the man into pulling the trigger. The gun might not work, but Christ, he thought, imagine, to come all this way, through just short of four decades, to sit in a hole like this and watch a total stranger blow his brains out. As a joke that would be pretty damn black.

But Duncan's perceived moment of glory shuffled back into the shadows and he lowered the weapon. As he did so, the light fled his eye, and he was ordinary again, nobody special, weak. He shambled to the door and returned the weapon to his jacket pocket, covering it with a grubby handkerchief kept there for the purpose.

At that moment Don returned, shoving the door back and pinning his flatmate against the wall. 'Whew, that's better! Got this dicky tummy lately, catches me off guard. Must be the smell of rubber.'

Duncan went to the table and sat down. Opened his tobacco tin and set about rolling a series of very thin cigarettes from its contents. Each one, upon completion, was squashed into the tin amidst the loose tobacco.

'Sad, isn't it,' Don said, slipping his jacket on again. 'He slopes back here after work, spends the evening rolling his fags for the next day, gets his head down, shimmies to the factory again, comes back, starts over. Stimulating or what?'

Duncan, crouching over his task, mumbled something incomprehensible. Don grinned at Will, assuming he would find the older man as entertaining as he did. Will's returned grin was weak.

'Now I really have to go,' Don said. 'If I'd known you were coming we could've made a night of it, but... fish to fry and all that.'

Following him to the door, Will glanced back. 'See you,' he said to the man at the table. Duncan, head bowed, eyes hooded, long, bony fingers moving slowly and methodically over the tobacco tin, gave no reply.

'What did you expect,' Don said, 'a hearty hug? Auld Lang fucking Syne?'

59

Steven Dornick went out so many evenings now that his work colleagues assumed that he'd gotten himself a woman at last, a local woman, a Brit. Either that or he couldn't keep away from the little sidestreet cathouse in Lakenheath village or the all-night massage parlor in Mildenhall that offered special rates for US service personnel. As Dornick had never struck them as a man in need of female company – any company really – the thought of him getting it out for a woman made him seem a tad more human. Dornick admitted nothing, denied nothing. Let 'em think what they want; anything but what I'm really doing off base.

While his visits to Cambridge were more regular now, every one so far had been a waste of time. When the woman was home her car was parked outside the house or in a nearby space. He'd seen her going in one other time and coming out twice. Frustratingly, it was always just her. The odd email nudge from Stoner hadn't helped.

'Are you still on it?'

'The mark hasn't showed yet or you'd have heard.'

And:

'The money's burning a hole. Any sign of him?'

'Wish there was. Can't be long now.'

That night the rain started as he was passing Newmarket. At first just a shower, within minutes it was bucketing down. He'd considered turning round, giving it up tonight, but being closer to Cambridge than the base by that time, he'd kept on. Reaching Alpha Road he parked the Nissan Micra fifty yards from the house, which was in darkness. The woman's car wasn't anywhere to be seen, which meant that she could come home any time. Maybe Tench would be with her. He decided to give it an hour at most.

When a small Fiat slipped into the space outside the house, he paid it little mind. It was just another car. But when a woman got out from the passenger's side he sat up; peered through the rain smacking the windshield. Her head was uncovered and even on such a night, by dull city lamplight, there was no mistaking that hair. All right, it wasn't her car – maybe hers had broken down or something – but she wasn't alone. The man who stepped out from the driver's side seemed more intent on not getting wet than she did, keeping his head down as he joined her on the sidewalk. The woman opened the little front gate; then the two of them were running up the path to the front door, laughing. Weird how running in rain makes people laugh. The woman put a key in the lock and went inside. A light came on. The man followed her in. Closed the door.

Well, Dornick thought. At last. Not the best kind of night for it, but it would have to do. Care must be taken in weather like this, though. Rain meant mud and the path round the side of the house wasn't paved; he might slip if he didn't watch out. He wasn't worried about leaving tracks. For these excursions he wore civilian shoes a size too big, bought well away from the base weeks ago. He *expected* to leave prints, size eleven prints that wouldn't match his size ten feet, and when he'd finished here he would dispose of the shoes in such a way that they would never be found – the Brügger & Thomet pistol too, and the trench coat he was wearing, the black fedora he would put on soon. Once out of the car, he would walk differently and hunch his shoulders, so that any description given, or image recorded by a hidden CCTV camera, wouldn't tally with the way he really walked and looked. No one, here or anywhere else, including those assholes on base, would associate him with the death of the sculptor.

But he didn't want to rush this. Rushing could lead to mistakes. He would wait a while, then climb in the window round the back. He would shoot Tench the moment he saw him, one to the body, one to the head, hoping the silencer lived up to its name unlike most of them. (Redner said the suppressor for the VP-9 was one of the best.) He would get out without a moment's delay, drive back to base by a circuitous route, always within the speed limit so as not to attract attention, stopping on the way to change his clothes, then sit back and wait for the screaming headlines and shortly after that see a million bucks in the account he'd set up in the Polish-sounding name of a bully he'd hated in Middle School.

Making himself comfortable in the cause of not rushing things, Dornick closed his eyes.

60

Colorless walls, glasses with traces of lipstick, smell of wet clothes from an unexpected downpour, big mirror behind the bar. The burly barman, hissing snakes tattooed along both hairy forearms, leans on the pump handles and watches a boxing match on the TV fixed to the wall, high up.

'Could I have one more?'

The barman turns. Dribbles a measure into the used glass.

'Make it a double.'

A sigh and a further measure. The blow-by-blow account of the middleweight bout is of more interest. In the darkest corner a white girl and a black lad have been quietly arguing. Now she's in tears. The roar of the TV drowns her sobs. The youth reaches for her hand. She snatches it away and a glass goes flying. The barman doesn't pay any attention. The lad glances up and catches Will's eye. Glares as if to say what are you looking at? Will looks away, finding refuge in the boxing match that he has absolutely no interest in. I must go, he thinks. Have to face her. Get it over with.

He downs the drink. Leaves.

61

For Wendy, the prospect of entertaining her as-yet-untried lover in a house that wasn't her own provided an exquisite air of detachment. She hadn't chosen the furniture, painted the walls, hung those pictures. Away from her own things and all reminders of Don, she felt capable of anything. Expectations of this turning into anything close to permanent were small, but if it proved to be nothing more than an isolated bit of fun, why not? If Don could do it – and he had, many times – why couldn't she? Why *shouldn't* she? Oliver wasn't hideous, he was considerate and thoughtful, had a good sense of humor. He held chairs out for her in restaurants and helped her on with her coat. Bit old fashioned, but that was kind of refreshing after the very different personality that had dominated her life for so long.

They'd gone to a small Italian restaurant and enjoyed twin mountains of straightforwardly good spaghetti. Wendy had wanted to pay for her half of the meal, but Oliver wouldn't hear of it. On the way to Nina's from there they had picked up a couple of bottles of wine, which again he insisted on paying for. He uncorked the first bottle in the comfort of the small front room as she picked out a few CDs and, with a smile, slid the first into the player. She turned off the main light, leaving only the flickering artificial coals of the fire. More than adequate, she thought. They sat together on the couch and listened to the music for a while, saying nothing. Her toes toyed with the large fluffy rug on the otherwise bare floorboards. 'Don't worry about the fake sheepskin,' Nina had said, 'I can always have it dry-cleaned if there's any spillage.'

'Why don't we lie there?' Wendy said.

62

Still raining but not as hard as it had been. Turning the corner into Alpha Road, his stomach churned. He reached the house. To the right of the front porch the bay window of the lounge, curtains drawn across, glowed faintly. He glanced around for their car. No sign. She must have parked along the street somewhere. Again he looked at the lounge window, again asked himself if he should have let her know he was coming, again failed to find an answer. He opened the gate, walked to the front door, stood in the porch trying to decide whether to ring the bell like a visitor or just go in. If she still felt the way she had when she stormed out, she might not appreciate his turning up out of the blue like this, out of the rain. But then he thought, No, sod it, I live here, and inserted his key.

Opening the door, the first thing he heard was music. A song that took him so much by surprise that he forgot his intention to call out rather than risk startling her with his unexpected presence. James Blunt? Nina playing James *Blunt*? The song was on a CD Wendy had given her years ago, a birthday present Nina had stared at incredulously on unwrapping it. 'Doesn't my sister know me at *all*?' So why would she play it now? Oh, wait. Part of a soundtrack of some film or TV show, has to be. He stood waiting for the song to give way to the dialogue of a drama or the narrative of a documentary. But it didn't give way, it carried on, through the walking out the door and up the street stuff, the looking at the stars falling down, the wondering where the singer went wrong, all the way to the end, whereupon, following a three or four second pause, another song began, another Blunt song. Will smirked. She's playing the whole *album*?

He shook some of the rain off and approached the lounge thinking no point calling out with little Jimmy Blunt shrieking away like that. He pushed the door back, increasing the new track's volume, half expecting to find her asleep on the couch. That would explain the album going on and on, if not how it got into the player in the first place. He didn't find her asleep, though. Or on the couch. The room's sole light was provided by the flickering coal-effect fire that had come with the house and never been replaced. In that light nothing was scrupulously illuminated, even the back of the naked woman with her arms out, as fully stretched as Bones of Golgotha's, astride a man whose face her body concealed as she eased herself up and down on him to the accompaniment of a song which, at any other time, she would do nothing but ridicule. Utterly stunned, Will had no reason to suppose that a woman with such hair, in that superficial fireglow, wasn't Nina. Who else could it be?

He backed out, pulled the door to with the exaggerated care of the drunk. The front door too, as if not wanting to disturb the serenaded couple. At the edge of the porch a gob of rain slithered down his neck, shaking him out of a budding trance and rushing him to the gate. In the street he stood a moment. The pavement was alive with fluid color, teased and stretched and broken by the rain. Far more color than he could use right now. He lunged at the palette-street, slicing a blade of rage through the shifting abstraction. Passed a parked Nissan Micra with a man asleep at the wheel.

63

Annoyed with himself for nodding off on this of all nights, he got out of the car and looked both ways along the wet street. Well spaced-out lamps the only illumination apart from the glow of curtained windows, nothing moving, no people about. He tugged his hat down, his coat collar up, and, heart beating a little faster than usual, hunched along to the house. There, very carefully, silently, he opened the side gate and slipped round the back. Total darkness. A small torch showed him anything he needed to see.

He went to the previously tested window which, huddling beneath the dripping overhang of the roof, he lifted soundlessly. After a slight listening pause he climbed in, in the process catching the brim of his hat on the window frame. The hat flew back and lay upturned beyond the overhang. Resisting the urge to go back for it – pick it up on the way out – he stepped down into the room. He didn't wipe his feet. No need to: those shoes would never be traced back to him.

A vertical strip of light from a mostly-closed door picked out a large dining table and four chairs sufficiently for him to avoid crashing into them. Crossing the room, he put an eye to the strip and peered into the hallway, far more nervous than he'd expected to be after so many mental run-throughs. Standing there, he couldn't miss the music issuing from a room off the hallway. The door of the room wasn't quite closed. A dim light showed around it. He tilted his head. No sound from above, no footsteps, creaking of floorboards, flushing of a toilet. What if they were both in that room? Or just the woman? If it was just her and she saw him, should he cut and run or... what? Fact was, there was no way of knowing who was in there without taking a look. He could only hope it was Tench, and that he was alone. He listened a moment longer. That song. One of his favorites.

He took out the gun. Checked it; armed it. It was ready. *He* was ready. Here, tonight, was the point of retribution for The Church of God's Great Light that he didn't give a holy shit about.

He was about to step forward when the song ended. He froze. His skin prickled. But then another track started. He nodded his head to the familiar beat. He liked that one too. Crossing the space between the two doors, he pushed the second back a fraction. The room's only illumination was supplied by a phony fire in the hearth, a poor light for most purposes but sufficient for him to see that both the man and the woman were there. They lay together on a white rug, on their sides, facing away from him, naked, the man's knees lodged into the backs of the woman's, one arm curled around her upper body. Dornick couldn't see the guy's face, but he didn't need to. Couldn't see hers either, but that was fine, it meant she couldn't see him. Quite a touching scene really. A couple at rest after lovemaking, lulled by the music. And the song? *Goodbye My Lover*.

He raised the pistol. His hand was not shaking. His nerves had settled. He'd come here for this, waited for it night after night, and suddenly everything was in place. He fired twice: once into the target's back, top left, once into his head, just behind his left ear. Two little jumps and the man was still.

So easy if you have the eye for it, Dornick thought.

He should have stepped back at once, but it's hard for a good marksman to turn from a perfect shot the instant it's made. Perfection should be admired, albeit briefly. Not briefly enough this time, however. The woman, startled not by the gun – the music had masked the muted *pfutt* of the silencer – but by the two sharp movements of her lover, glanced round, intending to query him, but instead saw Dornick in the doorway, about to back away. She stared, too nonplussed to be alarmed.

Jesus, she's seen me. She'll describe me.

The woman half sat up, throwing off the arm of the man who lay dead behind her. Dornick hesitated. That hair, even in this light it was glorious, and she had quite a body too. Eyes wide, staring at him, the gun in his hand, the woman on the sheepskin rug opened her mouth.

Oh no, not a scream. Please don't scream. They always do that in the movies. Don't scream.

Wendy didn't scream. The bullet in her mouth saw to that.

64

He'd had to wait over an hour for a train, and in Durham, three and a quarter hours later, a further hour and a half for the one that eventually delivered him to his destination. He'd dozed fitfully through much of the journey, but the three mile walk to Pendersdell and up to the house finished him. By the time he closed the door he felt as weary as if he hadn't slept for days, but even so, all these hours after the event, he was still haunted by what he'd seen in Cambridge. If Nina could do such a thing so soon after parting from him how did he know she hadn't done it before? It had rarely crossed his mind that she might, but on the way back he'd repeatedly run through the numerous occasions that he'd been absent: time enough, many times enough, for any number of opportunities. And all those night duties. Had she really been at the hospital every time? And the phone calls she'd tried to make on the hill and in the village. So frustrated that she couldn't get through. So angry. Now it seemed unlikely that Wendy had been the only person she'd wanted to contact. Contact? She'd wanted more than that. All the time they'd been up here she'd wanted to be with someone else.

Someone other than him. Someone she knew very well, in Cambridge. That wish would certainly account for the excessive brooding of late. That and the sudden departure from Bleakridge.

But now, sleep. His only requirement. And sleep he did, until the middle of the afternoon when, coming to, the memory of what he'd seen felt like nothing more than an unlikely concoction of the unconscious during slumber. Only as his head cleared did the concoction's veracity strike him full force, and then he came close to weeping. Pulling himself together as well as he could but needing to escape his thoughts, he went round the back of the house and jumped down onto one of the worn trails of dirt and gravel that wound round parts of the hill. You couldn't walk properly on these tracks, just stumble, slip, grab whatever you could to stop yourself tumbling sideways or down. Because of this he walked with his eyes mostly on the path immediately in front of him, but at one point he glanced up and saw, some way ahead, a figure, slightly blurred, that made his heart thump. Nina? No, can't be, not here, now. Wishing he had his specs with him he realized, all too slowly, that it wasn't Nina but the girl he'd taken for her more than once, standing there, just standing, lost in thought by the look of her. She didn't move as he drew closer. Continued to gaze out across the fields and woods and villages below and far away.

'Quite a view from here,' he said, just short of her.

She didn't answer; acknowledge him in any way. Nor did

she step aside to allow him to easily get by. He passed behind her, near enough to touch, which, suddenly, he very much wanted to do, for even up close she was so like Nina in their early years, if younger still.

When he returned to the house his mind was not on the girl, however, but the woman she resembled, and the anger surged back, anger seasoned with despair, a fragile combination that fueled hours of helplessness, hopelessness, aimlessness. The day dissolved about him, withered and folded so emptily that it might as well not have occurred. It wasn't yet dark when he started upstairs, but the staircase being in shadow he turned the light on. Before he'd taken three steps the bulb expired. He swore. The bathroom bulb had been replaced by a spare found in a kitchen cupboard, but there were no more spares.

In the bedroom he began to undress. He'd just thrown his trousers and pants onto the chair in the corner when he heard a small sound behind him. He jumped round. Blinked. The door appeared coarser than it should – older – and the floor dipped as if about to give way, and above him there wasn't a flat white ceiling but open rafters, darkening sky. He stood, a foolish figure in nothing but a shirt, on what remained of the moldering upper floor of the ramshackle structure he'd known as a boy. Disorientated rather than afraid, he reached wildly for something, anything, to keep from falling through the disintegrating floor, and at once the floor became solid again, the roof and ceiling intact, the door as it should be, as if self-correcting a silly mistake or careless lapse. Correct again or not, he jumped into bed, covered his head, and time passed, until he woke, pulled the duvet from his face, opened his eyes. Full night now. The moon in the only window cast its light on the lower third of the room, but in that light and the shadow above it a figure stood. Addled with sleep, he sat up.

'Nene?'

For answer, the woman shrugged off whatever it was she was wearing, a very loose garment, and stood naked in the half-light. She stepped forward, stooped to fold back the duvet, dropped to her knees beside the bed. For a moment the anger returned and he almost threw her off, but her hands were already on him, and when she bent her head he was lost. He reached for her hair, felt it around and between his fingers. She'd always been good at this, always. 'You've wasted your life,' he told her once. 'This has to be your top skill.'

She'd looked up. 'I'm a pretty good nurse.'

'Lucky patients. Don't stop.'

He could forgive her anything at such times, set aside all the differences, furious rows, recriminations, for the duration and a while afterwards. He could forgive her now, eyes closed, as his fingers laced her hair. But gradually, as the head continued to slowly move, the hair became less full, less soft, until it seemed to have no substance at all. He opened his eyes. The moonlight sprawled across his thighs, highlighting the head held lightly between his hands.

It wasn't Nina's. Wasn't any living person's.

It was a skull. A human skull. In whose lipless, tongueless, throatless mouth his penis rested.

65

The back roads he chose for his return this night, running between the flattest and dullest of fields, were far from regular or well-maintained. Used more by tractors and trucks than cars, they were pot-holed and pitted, uneven at best. The rain had turned the hunched shoulders of earth bordering the roads to mud, which spilled onto them. The night was as dark as a night can be, cloud-filled, no moon or stars, lights only in very distant, isolated windows. Yet the mood within the car was light, as the driver, seat belt cavalierly unfastened, joined in, full-throttle, with the 'la la la, la la la-la-la' chorus of *Can't Get You Out of My Head*, initially unaware when the front wheels failed to successfully navigate a renegade bump in the road, a failure that fostered a sharp skid and sequential collision with a stretch of ancient drystone wall that flew apart to allow the vehicle to flip over twice in the boggy field beyond, leaving the driver trapped inside, beneath something invisible and heavy, where Kylie's multi-million seller finally got out of his head, which had cracked open like an egg.

Even after the Micra's spin into that blankest of blank

fields the engine continued to run, allowing the radio to pump out singalong song after singalong song without a break. Lying there, unable to move a single part of himself, blood running into his eyes, not once in the five hours fourteen minutes left to him did Staff Sergeant Dornick join in a chorus. He had two last thoughts before his personal shutters came down for good. The first was that he hadn't collected the million bucks he'd worked for with such selfless dedication and boredom. The second and last was: 'Shit.'

66

He hadn't returned to bed. He'd shivered for what felt like hours, in a corner, on the floor, huddled within the duvet. At some point he fell asleep, and when he woke it was light. The skull lay where he'd thrown it in horror, beside the door, not quite looking his way. Coming to, he posed the obvious questions – 'How did it get here, did I bring it into the house, up here?' – and finding no answers dismissed the matter as he might an unsolvable conundrum. In the light of day the skull held few terrors. None really. He picked it up and took it downstairs. Placed it on the mantelpiece, like an ornament won at a fair.

He set about preparing for the day, distractedly at first, but gradually the anger recharged itself into a quivering fury that needed to be vented on a particular target. Vented the only way he could think of. He started with a meter-wide roll of craft paper scissored into lengths, which he set about with thick sticks of soft charcoal pastel, conjuring malformed representations of Nina the Betrayer. When he'd used up a dozen sheets he flipped through them, snarled with disgust, and bundled them out into the yard, where he burned them.

Watching the flames brought a momentary calm, but the anger soon returned, and he stalked back inside and set to work once more, again with the rich charcoal pastel but this time on canvas boards. Nina was still the main subject, sometimes clothed and standing but often naked, sprawling, legs spread. He gave himself up to an orgy of anguish in drawing after drawing, his every stroke an act of desecration, abuse, ridicule, as if Nina's continuing fidelity was all that he'd ever required of life. The resultant forms were tangled and twisted, their slashing lines as jagged as arbitrary gashes in flesh.

When he ran out of cheap surfaces to draw on he dashed paint onto the drawings without first bothering to fix the charcoal, in consequence of which it merged with or tainted the colors. He made no attempt to discriminate between colors, seizing a tube at random and using it until he felt in need of another, whose tint or hue would be as unimportant as its predecessor. Sometimes the mix worked, more often it did not, but as the colors were applied so they remained, scattering the dust of the charcoal this way and that, to good effect and bad. When each picture was as complete as he cared for it to be, he turned it away so as not to distract himself from the next, working on and on, picture after picture, invoking a cavalcade of rutting caricatures of Nina. Only when he realized that the latest picture was taking twice as long as earlier ones did he decide to finish for the day. He went to the bathroom and doused his head in cold water, then outside, for air and soft light.

Crossing the yard, he became aware of a rare sound, the thwop-thwop-thwop of whirling rotor blades, and looked up. The helicopter, evidently a sightseer chopper, bright yellow and black, paused for a handful of seconds, and in the pause he thought he saw a hand wave behind one of the high windows. He did not wave back, and the gaudy vehicle thwopped away in search of some other hill or landmark or solitary figure for its passengers to wave to.

He walked on, to the fence at the edge of the yard, and gazed down the hill. The young farmer was there, looking up, also at the helicopter perhaps.

67

There was no helicopter in Billy's sky as he glanced up from his work and saw the figure at the fence. The way the man stood, like it was his god-given right to be there; that he was master of Bleakridge. Billy resented that. Unlike the older folk, the young clods from Pendersdell still jeered at him; joked about his limp and all, those whelps who'd been too young to be conscripted, sent away from home to risk injury, disfigurement, death. He gave as good as he got with the village boys, chased them off and all; but this man, he was more of a threat than all the village lads stacked together, with his confident air and more. The 'more' included his hands all over Ella that time at the river. No need to wonder what was on his mind then. And now? Was she why he came here without a by-your-leave? Whatever else I might let go, Billy thought, he's not getting Ella. Ella's mine. Mine alone.

But he did not leave his work and storm up the hill to the house. Not that time. Somehow... somehow his heart wasn't in it. Wasn't in anything much just then.

68

My tongue between the thighs of someone else's dream.
Might have been someone else's, might not, but nothing felt
quite his on waking. Everything he'd ever experienced, seen,
felt, suddenly seemed ripe for the taking. So he got going,
drawing and painting anything that came to mind or hovered
on the periphery, delighting in extreme distortion, whipping
up interiors like the drawstrings of a canvas bag, leaving
their occupants, if any, on heaving floors, reaching for walls
that leaned away, windows too fluid to be opened. He
invoked a lot of windows. Rotting frames, dangling sashes,
broken panes through which neighboring gardens were
merely hinted at.

In charcoal and paint he recalled rooms of rowdy
students, the lugubrious gardener who turned out to be a
defrocked priest, the seedy middle-aged couple who always
went to a boarding house's only bathroom together and
stayed in there for an age, the Roman magistrate's daughter
who made such a racket during sex, and the older woman,
more than three times his age at the time, who said 'Will you
cum on my face?', and after the cumming the going, with

smiles and hugs. Others too before Nina, not many, and none after, but many a situation, setting, address – dripping taps, stains on ceilings, cracks on walls, faded lampshades – all this and more, much more, went into pictures made over that and the following days, with short breaks between, food breaks, bathroom breaks, sleep breaks, as a routine of sorts established itself.

Hopping back and forth between the boundaries of his thirty-nine years, he referred now to an incident that had taken place a year ago, now to one from boyhood. Unrelated fragments of his life overlapped and quickly supplanted one another in no sensible order. Far too often his mind was an agitated, amorphous realm where fancy, memory and reality coalesced, leaving no recognizably sane separation point. So it was that, as he worked – and slept – he set aside without intending to his grip on the day-to-day, the here-and-now. He was eleven again, and twenty-five, and thirty-one, and eighteen, and each age carried its own soiled sack of images and errors, fantasies and flaws.

As the days passed and he worked on, through image after image, he recalled the so-soft flannel his grandmother washed him with when he was small, sitting on the kitchen table. His grandparents appeared in several pictures, as jovial heads whose bodies trailed away to almost nothing, or fussing giants with prematurely lined faces, or keeling over into brilliant garden blooms, scattering insects. His mother was there too, but a vague, virtually faceless figure, for his memories of her were few and slight, and it still hurt, intermittently, secretly, that she'd abandoned him at such a tender age and never communicated with him again. And his father, his dad, representations of him showed a gloomy figure in his cups, alone in one of those wildly lurching rooms or in rain-sodden streets, and finally his drunken face striking sparks off a live rail. In this last there was a background figure, a wide-eyed boy with theatrically-raised hands, an expression of horror tempered by an utterly calm mouth. He made images of people he'd known or seen in environments he'd thought forgotten: schoolfriends and teachers, bosses and co-workers; the Scottish waitress in a seaside hotel who had a profile straight out of classical Greece; the one-legged tramp tripped over in Piccadilly Circus one Christmas who turned out to be dead.

For a time he eschewed representations of Nina, but every so often she appeared in one guise or another. She'd been so much a part of his life, for so long, that she couldn't easily be dismissed or detached from it, but now she was just another subject and as such he returned her to many of the settings they'd known together, in a range of stances, attitudes, moods. She was topless on a foreign beach; laden with sweaters during an icy winter; doubled over with one foot in a high washbasin; alarmed by a rat racing from a skirting board. He depicted the two of them together on a hillside or standing apart in the shadow of some ruin, kicking leaves along a country lane, discovering a dead sheep trapped in a wire fence in Wales, bluebottles dining out on its eyes. There was a small back kitchen in one of their early flats where she stood ironing while he lolled idly; there were baths together, and other scenes of intimacy. Tiny memories flooded back during all this: burnt meals, unwanted visitors, letters from bank managers, book club literature they couldn't resist, mail-order catalogues that they could.

Intermittently, as the days passed, he questioned his hold on reality, his sense of place and time. It was nineteen-eighty something and he was a kid again, and then it was now, and he was still a kid. Often the scenery was shaky too, in both past and present, but hadn't it always been thus? You turn round, half round, and something's different, but blink, and it's just right again, or at least acceptable enough to move on from. Is it like this for everyone or must you possess (or lack) a certain kind of mind? Does this inability to maintain your grip on the what, the why, the where equate to some sort of mental imbalance, or is it simply a side-effect born of cognitive solitude? Whatever it is, whatever it's *ever* been, should it be a cause for concern or merely a condition to be endured, indulged perhaps? He preferred the latter view; presented it to himself as an abstract conclusion and just got on with things, not exactly whistling while he worked but more at ease than before, with himself, his surroundings, all that was and quite possibly wasn't.

Along with so many other things, he depicted the house, Bleakridge, inside and out, in all the phases of its existence that he could recall or imagine. Often the phases overlapped. The house heaved and changed, crumbled, rose again, groaned with age and confusion. It might have a lean-to shed or an outside privy, there might be chickens in the yard, or an old car parked near the door, or a horse and cart. In its semi-ruined state there were nettles all across the floor, wall to wall like a great bed, a stinging bed. Windows would reflect charcoal clouds. There might be a figure in one of them, a faceless shape gazing out. Sometimes a boy would stand on the fallen door, peering in. Inside, other boys would be scribbling on the walls, or masturbating, excited by their participation in the corruption of the place. In one picture of the interior he painted a man hanging from the main beam, by the neck. He had no idea where that came from.

Only one individual stood in sunlight. Stood or danced as it spiraled down through the shattered roof of a ruin. He thought of her as Nina, but she was younger than Nina, with wilder hair. Calmer than today's Nina too, with a less severe expression. While recreating her within such walls, rivals for her attention, her body, mouth, ceased to be important: incidental figures easily shrugged off, or painted out.

He didn't count the young farmer as a rival. Sometimes, taking a breather, he would see him on the side of the hill, going through the motions of working, and call out a greeting. The lad never replied. Once, though, once, stretching his legs in a stroll round the outside of the house, he turned a corner and the farmer came at him with something in his hand that might have been a weapon of some kind. Will crashed back against the wall.

But an instant later he was alone.

69

When the attack came it surprised him. Shocked him. He'd
been shoring up a weak patch in the east wall of the house
and was on his way to put his tools under cover when the
incomer lurched round the corner and almost sent him
sprawling. He was gone at once, but after that Billy was
wary; half expecting to be confronted by the man every time
he turned a corner.

One day, while working down below, he again saw him
up there by the fence, and decided to have words. He
dropped everything and stormed up, but when he got there,
there was no sign of the man. He was nowhere, not in the
yard or the house or on any side of the hill. Ella was, and she
swore she'd seen no one. Billy looked hard at her. She
seemed sincere.

70

Making do as far as possible with his store of non-perishable foodstuffs, he went down to the village shop only when necessary, always tidying himself up to conceal the kind of work he was doing.

'How's the book coming along?' Mrs. Temple asked across the counter on one occasion.

'Slowly,' he said. Standard response to such enquiries.

He had ordered more materials from the art shop by way of the phone at the pub, and they'd been delivered and he'd used most of them up. Pictures stood against every wall, leant against table legs, chairs, one another, turned away, every one of them, so that their images could not be seen. Time enough to look at them, something else to do first, for another kind of harking back had seized him, to sculptures and carvings from that vast unrecorded hinterland of time conveniently labeled human prehistory: artifacts that had so captivated him as an archaeological illustrator and subsequent sculptor. Working mainly out of doors because of the space required, he constructed a series of wire armatures, vaguely humanoid in shape and contour, a meter to a meter and a half in height, varying in girth. He then wrapped the armatures in scrim, onto which he slapped ready-made industrial plaster from the big tubs that stood along the front wall. From time to time he would reach into one of the emerging figures, haul out a wire section and distort it in imitation of a malformed limb, then cover that too. Preferring coarse textures to smooth, if any of them seemed too clearly defined or delicate, he roughened the surface and bullied areas into less obvious directions or positions. Being neither monolithic nor megalithic in size, scale or character, at some point during their construction he began thinking of the figures, with some amusement, as miniliths. Completed, they stood haphazardly around the yard, not quite human in demeanor yet appearing to stare eyelessly at him or the house or out from the hill, depending on which way they were facing.

Just below the fence on that small piece of land which was flatter than any other part of the hill, he dug fourteen holes about thirty centimeters deep, in a circle roughly five meters in diameter, and into the holes set his miniliths, facing center, as the constituent parts of a Neolithic or Bronze Age stone ring might. Only when he'd positioned the last but one did he realize that he'd miscounted. He'd dug fourteen holes but made only thirteen miniliths. He had just enough wire, scrim and plaster for another, but the impulse to make more was gone.

Next day, the plaster being sufficiently hardened, he set

about coloring the thirteen bone-white figures, splashing paint onto them or rubbing it into them, coloring them earth and autumn, old bronze and stone. Another year, he thought, and they'll look as if they've stood here for centuries. They wouldn't last centuries, of course. Eighteen months maybe, before the plaster started to crumble or flake off here and there. And, of course, some vocal local might consider them an eyesore, and agitate for their removal. But as he wouldn't be there to witness either development, he didn't care what might become of the things. He'd made them, brought them into being, and that was sufficient.

71

Some nights, without announcing that he was going to, Billy slept in blankets by the hearth. The cooling embers in the grate were warmer than the company in his bed. Months had passed since the awful event of the suit and tie. Ella had barely let him touch her since then; certainly not encouraged him to. The odd peck on the cheek, squeeze of an arm, from her or from him, and that was it. He wanted so much more. Wanted to kiss her mouth, kiss her all over, hold her properly, but whenever he approached her with such things in mind he thought he detected a hint of distaste in her expression, and held back.

In spite of her attitude, her increasingly plain disdain for him, Ella was never far from his thoughts, whether he was with her or not. He longed for her. Her flesh, her touch, the various parts of her; but the sight of her, the *clothed* sight, was all there was now. He wrote poems about the way she looked, the way he felt about her, his dreams of her, how much he wanted her. He put the Ella poems in the Poetry Box in the small back cupboard under the stairs. He never mentioned that he'd written them, that he'd written any poems at all, sure that she, like his father, would ridicule him for wasting his time on such nonsense.

Thus he wrote and brooded the months away, turning ever more in upon himself, beleaguered by unexpressed bitterness, humiliation, thwarted desire. The anguish of this coupled with his grinding, thankless existence brought him often to the brink of despair, but only he knew it. Ella went off for hours on end and never said where she was going or where she'd been. He always thought the worst but never mentioned it, and the rooks from the spinney down below circled the hill like hungry vultures awaiting their moment, and Bleakridge mocked him with its stillness, its shadows, its silence.

72

He heard the post van while still in bed. Post was no big event. There was never anything for him. There wouldn't be as no one knew this address, or the name he went by here. Very occasionally there was something for Mr. and Mrs. Morley or for someone he'd never heard of – a previous owner, perhaps – but mostly it was junk mail. Letters or junk, these days he always scooped it up without a glance and shoved it in a kitchen drawer. Not long ago the post had included one for Mr. Keating, postmarked Cambridge, but he hadn't noticed it as he gathered and deposited the envelopes.

Getting up today, he knew that he'd done all that he could. There was nothing more that he wanted to depict or construct. It felt surprisingly good to be without inspiration or creative desire. After breakfasting on his usual toast and coffee, he eyed the accumulation of used crocks and cutlery. So much, so many, in the sink, on the draining board, all other surfaces. He set about washing and drying, washing and drying, a seemingly endless task. Returning to the main room at last, he looked at all that mess too, and the multitude of canvases and boards facing the walls like scolded children. He wasn't yet tempted to turn them round. Many would be ugly, inept, good for nothing but burning. He'd painted with such speed, so little care, especially in the beginning, that he couldn't remember the content of most of them. He would look at them later, or tomorrow, after he'd returned the house to a reasonably civilized state. Today was clean-up day, for the house and himself.

Running a bath, he inspected himself in the mirror over the basin. In the glass, the shallow lines on his face were emphasized by charcoal and smeared paint. His hair was thick with paint and plaster, swept back as if by a hand dipped in multi-colored wax. The hot water in the bath steamed the mirror up, improving the reflection no end, but he cleared it away to sufficient extent to get to work on his beard and hair. The stuff in his hair wouldn't wash out now it was dry. So thickly larded was it that he had to cut it out, and having started he couldn't stop. When he'd finished he looked as if he'd visited a prison barber with a grudge.

Stripping off, he got into the bath, stretched out as well as he could within its limitations, remained there for some time enjoying the warmth, the stillness, a rare sense of calm. Drying himself on the last reasonably clean towel, he wished he'd thought to light a fire to go out to. He also hadn't thought to look out a change of clothes and in nothing but the towel, already shivering, he went upstairs to find some. Once dressed, he set about clearing the grate in the main room and building a fresh fire, using up the last of the peat and bracken he'd previously piled into the large chest in the lean-to. Only when the fire was set did he realize that he had nothing to light it with. Formerly he'd lit rolled sheets of paper on a ring of the cooker in the kitchen, but the gas bottle that fueled the cooker had run out. He went down to the village for matches. At the shop he also bought bread, cheese, an assortment of microwaveable meals, and five bottles, each containing a different kind of alcohol.

Heading back up the hill, cursing the weight of the bottles, he was surprised to see an unfamiliar kitchen chair lying beside the track. Sure that it hadn't been there on the way down, puzzled as to where it could have come from in the interim, he looked back several paces on and, once again, it wasn't there. The chair's disappearance might have startled him had not something occurred to him a moment later that achieved more prominence. That of all the subjects he'd chosen to draw and paint there was one that he hadn't so much as considered: the threat on his life that had brought him and Nina here. So amazed was he that he hadn't thought to depict this in some form that by the time he reached the house it was the one thing he felt he really had to do. He lit the fire, squatted before it for a time, watching the flames gather and grow. Then he opened the first of the bottles with a view to opening the others in pretty short order as the day progressed. *If I'm going to get hammered I might as well mix my drinks.*

There was still some paper left to work on, and a few

pieces of board. As before, he began with charcoal drawings: absurd distortions of amorphous fabrications that seemed appropriate to the theme. When he ran out of clean surfaces he lashed black and brown paint on the back of some of the canvases he hadn't yet looked at, forging images that included crosses, nails, guns, bared teeth and mad eyes, their grimness intermittently relieved by bright splashes of red, yellow, green.

In all these weeks he'd given little thought to the creation that had so agitated The Church of God's Great Light in Mississippi. The piece hadn't meant much to him at the time of its construction. Little more than a joke really, he wouldn't have cared if someone had smashed it to bits, or if it had become an object of ridicule – a chorus that he might, in the right frame of mind, have joined in with. He hadn't said as much in the three interviews (two radio, one TV) that he'd been offered following Bones of Golgotha's shortlisting for the Turner. In one, asked about the powdery white content of the condoms hanging from the crucified figure, he'd let them think, without actually confirming it, that it was his own semen. It wasn't. It wasn't anyone's. It was powdered milk, soaked in a little water then left to dry in the rubbers. 'And the significance of the twelve condoms?' another interviewer had asked. 'I'll leave that for you to decide,' he'd answered, having given no thought whatever to their significance, mainly because there was none.

Throughout the afternoon, while he worked he drank

straight from the bottle. Four of the five bottles were screwtops. One had a cork. Annoyed when he couldn't immediately find a corkscrew for this, he finally located a large, very antiquated one at the back of the cutlery drawer in the kitchen: a vicious-looking 1920s Darly with a fiercely twisted and pointed screw. Extracting the cork with this, he tossed the Darly onto the table, where it agitated for a place among the less aggressive tools, brushes and paints he'd been using.

By late afternoon the fire had gone out without his noticing. His hand remained steady enough in spite of the drink, but as his mind became less focused his imagination expanded, so that as the day began to fade and it became necessary to turn the lights on, the images he produced, while more controlled than before, seemed to his increasingly uncritical eye more authentic, if no more realistic. Realism had no more place here than perfection.

Working hour after hour on picture after picture he missed just one thing. Music. At home, in his studio, he usually worked to music of various kinds delivered by an iPod connected to external speakers. Having no musical devices here, the silence seemed absolute. It was thanks to this that when a car chugged into the yard after struggling up the hill, he couldn't fail to hear it.

He froze. Listened. Who could it be? Not Nina. Could it? The doorbell rang. He set his brush aside and stared at the closed door, trying to come to terms with what Nina's return might mean. After what he'd seen in Cambridge he could hardly welcome her. Couldn't let her simply walk back in as if nothing had happened. But if he did, if he pretended to have been here at the time and seen nothing, would she tell him about it out of guilt or something of the kind? If she did, what would he do? What *should* he do, forgive and forget? Kick the image of her and her lover out of his mind? Could he do that? Wasn't it burned into his brain for good and all? Would there be years with her in which he carried that picture of her sitting astride the man, arms outstretched as she rose and fell on him with such demonstrable pleasure?

The bell again.

No clearer in his mind as to what he might do faced with Nina and either the truth or no mention of it, he went to the door. Opening it, the only light that fell on the person standing there came from the room itself, around Will's own shadow.

'Mr. Keating?'

Struggling to lose those alternative futures with Nina, he did not answer immediately. The young man before him was American. Even with just two words spoken, four syllables, his accent made that clear if his clothing did not. He wore a loose jacket, in the right breast pocket of which Will detected, even in his own shadow, a significant bulge, and, on one of the jacket's lapels, a small badge in the shape of a fish.

73

'Lady at the little store down in the village gave me your name,' the young man said. 'Sorry to intrude, kinda dark out here, so a stranger on your doorstep might not be entirely welcome. I could come back in the morning if it's more convenient.'

'The morning?' Will managed.

'Sure, if it suits you better. Yeah, I'll come back tomorrow, sorry again for disturbing you.'

As he turned away, Will said: 'What is it you wanted?'

The man paused. 'I was going to ask if I could take some pictures. Of the house. Some outside ones, though it's too dark for those now, but a few inside ones too, if you'll allow it.'

'What do you want pictures of the house for?'

'Well, it's William's. Was, that is, I guess.'

'William's?'

'William Rainey. I'm hoping to do a little bio of him. Lots to find out yet, but...' Apparently intrigued by Will's puzzlement, he said: 'You know William Rainey, of course?'

Will shook his head. 'Never heard of him.'

'Jeez,' his visitor said. 'You live here, and you...?'

He let the rest go in a show of amazement. They stood before one another in the half light, half shadow. The first of the night's stars were visible behind the American's head. Behind Will was the riot of images produced in the past few hours: representations of danger, murder, fear.

'Evert Mildren.'

He frowned at the proffered hand. 'Sorry?'

'My name. Evert Mildren. Good to meet you, Mr. Keating.'

Will gripped his visitor's hand lightly, but withdrew it sharply as he realized that the act of doing so could give him the opportunity to reach into his pocket with his free hand.

'I would have called before coming up,' Mildren said, 'but the lady at the store didn't have a number for you.'

'She wouldn't have,' Will said.

'You really don't know of William Rainey?' Another head shake. 'Well now.' A pause, before: 'I don't suppose I might come in for a minute?' Will said nothing. 'Or if you prefer, like I said I could come back tomorrow, or even the day after that. I only have three more days – should have allowed more time, I guess – my plane leaves for Columbus, four p.m. Thursday.'

'Columbus?'

'Columbus, Mississippi.'

'Oh,' Will said, 'Mississippi,' which confirmed everything. His brain was both racing and sluggish, clear and confused. *What do I do? What?* 'Give me a minute,' he said.

He closed the door, threw the bolt, pulled the curtains across the main window. He stepped away from the window, and the door. He had no doubt what the man was really here for. They'd tracked him down. So much for the anonymous picture in the press and on TV, the false name, not telling anyone where he was. So, scenario in the next few minutes? The man either takes a handful of random shots through the door in the hope of hitting me or I let him in and he shoots me in his own time. And I do what? Just let it happen? Take the bullet, maybe two, three, and that's it, end of story, my story? Fine ending. My life in pictures all around my bullet-ridden body. More witty headlines for the tabloids.

But suppose I let him in, don't let on that I know what he's here for, string him along a bit...

He heard the car start up and sprang to the door, withdrew the bolt.

'Wait!'

Mildren wound his window down.

'You'd better come in,' Will said. 'Sorry, wasn't expecting anyone. Don't get visitors up here much, and... you know... the dark....'

Mildren turned the engine off, unclipped, got out. 'Are you sure? I really could come back.'

'No, it's fine, come in.'

'Well, I appreciate that. Thanks.'

Will ushered him inside, determined about one thing if

nothing else, to keep the man in his sights, not turn his back for a moment. A moment was all it would take for him to get that gun out.

'Wow!' Mildren said as he entered. 'Whatever I expected it wasn't anything like this. These are yours?'

Will grunted. Closed the door, sealing them both in.

Mildren approached the nearest of the pictures depicting the threat that had brought Will here. He looked twenty-eight, maybe thirty, had short dark hair, was clean shaven, casually dressed. Nothing unusual about him, nothing suspicious or alarming, but demeanor aside all the signs were there of his true intent: the bulge in his jacket pocket, the Christian symbol on his lapel, his place of origin in the US.

'Strong stuff,' Mildren said of the pictures. 'Kinda nightmarish. Is it okay to call them that?'

'Call 'em whatever you want.'

'Is there a story behind them?'

'How do you mean, story?'

'I mean there's a lot of menace in them. Menace and... so many crosses.'

'You said something about someone who used to live here.'

'Oh, yes,' Mildren said. 'Apologies. Your pictures kind of...' He struggled for words that didn't come.

'Took your mind off your purpose?'

A small laugh. 'I guess.' He became more businesslike.

'William Rainey, sorta hero of mine. Me and a few others back home. British poet. English, I should say.'

'Poet? Lived here? This house?'

'Yeah, back before World War Two, and after it, not sure how much after. Wrote wonderful poems about life here, and the war, but my favorites are the love poems to an unnamed woman. He describes the way she laughs, moves, looks. Heartfelt work.'

'What was the name again?'

'Evert, Evert Mildren.'

'Your poet's.'

'William Rainey.'

'My knowledge of British poets, any poets, is very limited.'

'Oh, he's not well known,' Mildren said. 'Not even published in the commercial sense, far as I know.'

'Then how...'

'A box of his poems – hand-written, three to four hundred of them – have been in my family since the late nineteen-seventies. The first owner was my grandfather, but it was his daughter, my mother, who really loved them and got me into them. Mom's been saying for so long how she wanted to find out about William, but there's nothing about him anywhere that we've seen, even online. We only got this address because he wrote it on some of the poems.'

While giving the impression that he was taking all this in, Will paid scant attention to the tale. It was spurious, of course, a concoction, either rehearsed in advance or made up on the spot, to lull him, and when he was sufficiently lulled, the kid would whip that gun out, do what he came to do, then go on his way and claim his holy blood money.

'And this is it,' Mildren said, gazing around once more. 'This is where he lived. I can't tell you what a thrill it is to be here. Is this all of it? The entire place?'

'A couple of small rooms upstairs,' Will said, 'and a tiny kitchen through there, but that's it.'

'No bathroom?'

'Beyond those slats. This room was bigger once.'

'Bigger?'

'The bathroom cuts into it.'

'Oh, you know the house from sometime before?'

'A little.'

'How long have you owned it?'

'I don't own it. I'm renting it. Temporarily.'

'Really? The owner then, does he live locally?'

'It's a couple. They moved away.'

'I wonder if they know the history of the place?'

'Can't say, I've never met them.'

'I should have waited til tomorrow,' Mildren said. 'Not sure my camera'll make much of the light in here – if you'll even let me take pictures, that is.'

'You wouldn't want photos with all my stuff about,' Will said.

'Well, I could hardly ask you to put it away, could I?'

'No. You couldn't.'

'I just need something to take home for my mom. She'll be so disappointed if I go back with nothing. But I'll still need some daylight shots of the outside.'

'So like you said, come back tomorrow.'

'Yeah, guess that would be the thing to do. I wonder if I might use your bathroom before I go?'

Will nodded toward the bathroom. Mildren smiled his thanks, opened the door, found the light cord, went in.

Will stared at the closed door. This was it. He'll be getting his gun out in there, checking it, ready for when he comes out, expecting me to be just standing here, suspecting nothing, and bang-bang, job done, and he drives down the hill, and away, and it could be weeks before anyone finds me. The curtain's drawn. The postman will think nothing of that. Sleeping late, he'll think. By the time someone does think to investigate, the place will stink. Stink of me, rotting on the floor surrounded by all these pictures of violence, brutality, fear. Perfect setting, really.

He heard the toilet flush. He knelt down, peered up through the slats of the door. As you could see out of the bathroom more clearly than you could see in, it was a risk, but he could see his visitor, just about, and he was turned away, washing his hands. Then he was drying them on the towel and reaching inside his jacket. *He's getting ready to deal with me. I have minutes to live. Moments.*

He jumped up, went to the front door, started out,

intending to get the hell away from there – but stopped. Considered. *There's an alternative.* He whirled about, ran back inside leaving the door open, snatched an implement from among the painting and drawing materials on the table, and positioned himself beside the bathroom door an instant before it opened. Mildren came out. Will leapt at him. Drove the old Darly corkscrew deep into his neck. Gasp of surprise, shock, pain. Mildren sagged. Will fell upon him, plunged the corkscrew into his neck again, pulled it out, rammed its vicious point into his cheek, then his right eye, with a frenzy that might have come directly from many of the surrounding images. Mildren made no sound beyond that initial gasp other than his last, a bubbling sort of cry as blood burst from his mouth, nose, eye. He lay there, half his face red, the other half yellowed by the room's artificial light. The fingers of one hand twitched, then ceased to move at all.

Will got to his feet, tossed the corkscrew away, grabbed a bottle from the table. He tipped it to his mouth, swallowed until it was empty, then dropped it. The bottle landed on the chest of the dead man, rolled off, away. He did not move for some time. Might have remained there longer still had not the light bulb in the ceiling flickered, flickered again, and gone out. He didn't curse, didn't think about ropy wiring, as he had when the staircase bulb went, but merely stood there as night poured in the open door, a slow tide of darkness that swept over him, consumed him.

74

It was one of those foggy, confused awakenings laced with worry that the chaos lingering in the mind might not be the stuff of dreams. He was still dressed, so he headed downstairs at once, but about to turn the stairs at the bottom, he paused. A dream or not? And then he looked. Saw the spreadeagled body. He sat down hard on the last step but one, gaping across the room at the dead assassin on the floor.

After a time, when the actuality of it had truly sunk in, he got up and went to the body. The face was hideous, its expression somewhere between fear and astonishment, with one eye open, staring blankly, the other skewered, dried blood trailing from it, down the cheek, to the floor. For many moments Will merely stood, merely looked, but at last he shook himself, snatched a bundle of discarded cloths from the floor, and covered the ruined face. Then, squatting down beside the body, he reached inside the jacket, to the right breast pocket. Expecting to find a weapon, he drew out a small hardback book. Gold lettering on a malachite green cover:

ON THE BLEAK RIDGE
The Poems of William Rainey

He tossed the book aside and went through the other pockets. He found an American passport, a wallet with a little money in it, a plane ticket, little else. No gun. No weapon of any kind.

He got up, went outside, to Mildren's car, a rented blue Honda. In the boot he found an unlocked suitcase containing clothes, toiletries, a digital camera, papers. Among the papers were research notes on the poet William Rainey.

He stood back from the car. 'What have I done?' he whispered, unnecessarily.

75

Sunday. A fine but extensive mist concealed the village roofs that could be seen from the fence on clear days, which meant that no part of Bleakridge would be visible from down there either. He took a spade to the plateau below the fence, and deepened and widened the hole he'd dug for the non-existent fourteenth sculpture. He then carried down what was left of the scrim and the half-empty last tub of plaster, and finally lugged Mildren's body down. The body was far heavier than the miniliths. Touching it induced no horror or disgust now that he'd got used to the fact of it.

Bringing Mildren's knees up to his chest, he roped his legs tightly to the torso and maneuvered the folded body into the widened hole, in an upright position so that the bulk of it was above ground. He wound the scrim around the squatting body, like a bandage, and lashed plaster onto it, very thickly in parts so as to reduce its resemblance to an actual person. Once the head and body were concealed, he rubbed small stones and soil into the plaster to coarsen the look of it.

Returning to the house, he took the drawings and paintings made the day before and burnt them in the yard, thereby, in his mind, disposing of the threat that had inspired them. He also burnt all of Mildren's effects and papers, and in the first darkness of evening drove the Honda quietly down the track and round the near side of the village, where there were few properties. Many miles away, along an unbeaten track discovered some days before Nina's departure, he nosed the car into a long-abandoned, very overgrown copse at whose heart tumbled the last vestiges of a small nineteenth century brick kiln. Leaving the car there, locked, he threw the keys as far as he could into undergrowth. Walking away, he visualized the hackneyed scene from so many films, in which the villain or hero, having tossed a match into a vehicle, strolls toward the camera in slo-mo, cool as you like, not even blinking when the vehicle becomes a ball of fire behind him. *Pity I didn't think to bring the matches.* Something else he hadn't thought of was to wipe his fingerprints off those parts of the car that he'd touched. By the time this occurred to him he was too far away – not relishing the long walk still ahead – to return to the car and wipe it clean of prints.

It took him over two hours to get back to Bleakridge in the dark. Two hours in which he saw no one, no light or car, no property that wasn't ruined. Sleeping late next day, his first act on dressing was to check the plaster on Mildren's body. It was surface-dry, as expected, so he colored it until it looked sufficiently like its companions in the circle. It was bulkier than the others, but not outrageously so. In the afternoon he went down to the shop on the pretext of buying bacon, though he had no means to cook it, and engaged Mrs. Temple in a casual conversation that elicited a question from her about a young American who'd said he wanted to call on him.

'An American?' he said. 'When was this?'

'Saturday. Long after closing, but I was about.'

'Well, he didn't visit me, or if he did I missed him. I did pop out for an hour or so on Saturday, just for a walk, stretching my legs.'

'It was quite late,' Mrs. Temple said. 'Getting dark.'

'That could be it then. It was completely dark by the time I got back. Did he say what he wanted?'

'Something about some poet that used to live there, at Bleakridge.'

'A poet?'

'Oh, way before our time.'

'A poet at Bleakridge, eh? Hard to imagine.'

Mrs. Temple agreed. 'Still, you writers...'

Will laughed. 'Yes, us writers. Funny lot.'

'You said it, not me.'

She was still chuckling when he left the shop.

76

By the following day, a dull overcast day that threatened rain, the American had ceased to exist even in memory. He was just one more figure on a hillside. This was the day he decided he would view the paintings produced these past weeks. He had painted them impulsively, hastily, without giving much of a damn for finer points, details, quality, and he wanted to see all of them at once; come upon them as a stranger might, head full of anything but their possible imagery. The plan was to turn them round without looking at them, leave the house, and come back in a while to gaze upon them as if for the first time. It was a way of viewing his work that he'd fallen into in his pre-sculpture days: finishing a painting to his relative satisfaction then leaving it, to look at hours or days later with a degree of detachment.

He put it off til the afternoon, fiddling with things that didn't really need doing or seeing to, but eventually began turning the pictures round, intent on avoiding any but the most cursory glance. It was soon clear that there wasn't enough space to display all of them at once, less than half perhaps, ranged on every level, at every angle, on the lower stairs, on cupboards and chairs, leaning against table legs, walls, doors. The first crop of boards and canvases exposed everywhere he might turn, it was difficult to keep his eye from lingering here and there, but he resisted for the most part, and grabbed his jacket, went out, headed down the track to the foot of the hill, and past the spinney, into Pendersdell village.

77

Colin walked across the steep slope of the hill trying to keep his body upright by bending his right leg and keeping his left straight. 'Where you off to?' his mother had wanted to know. He'd told her he was going to Eddie Wignall's and that had satisfied her, but really he'd just wanted to get out of the house, away from the bar. Specially the bar. He couldn't stand all those loud voices, the laughter, the stink of beer, Mum playing up to the men like some tart off the telly. The last person he wanted to see was that little creep Wignall.

He stopped. The man renting Bleakridge was no more than twenty yards away, walking down the track. Colin dropped to the ground, flattened himself against it. When he lifted his head the man was almost in the village. Where was he going? The shop or the Duck, that's all there was. If the Duck he might be there for hours, but if it was the shop he could be on his way back in minutes. Assuming that it might be the shop, he scrambled up the hill with more haste than was wise given the slope of it, grabbing ragged fistfuls of grass to keep from slipping back. Making it to the flat apron of land just below the house, he stared briefly at the circle of not-quite-human figures – *What the hell?* – before reaching up and climbing over the fence into the yard, where he glanced down to make sure no one was coming, or watching.

Nervous about being at the house even if the man was out, Colin shaded his reflection against the window beside the door. Hard to see much in there, but he caught no movement. There shouldn't be if the woman wasn't there, but there was still the thought that she could be, even though there was no car in the yard – or someone else, perhaps; someone he didn't know about.

Summoning his nerve, he tried the door, not really expecting it to be unlocked, surprised to find that it was. He pushed it back a bit, called out on the off chance. Receiving no reply he went in, leaving the door ajar. He didn't turn the light on, didn't dare, but as his eyes adjusted to the gloom he gasped. There were pictures everywhere, paintings, more than he'd ever seen in one place. Mad pictures of rooms with wonky walls, wobbly doors and windows. Not a straight line among them. There were people in many of them, with sickly faces, staring eyes, weird bodies. Dad had said the man renting Bleakridge was some sort of writer, so what was all this? Maybe his wife had painted them. Yes, now that he thought of it, she looked kind of like the woman in some of them. Pictures of herself then, often without a stitch on, legs all over the place, doing stuff, or having stuff done to her.

Holy shit.

78

The funeral of Wendy's lover had taken place five days ago. Nina had not attended it. She could imagine the horror of his family, whatever family he had, upon hearing that his naked body had been found entwined with that of a woman they'd never heard of, in the home of the sculptor who'd achieved brief notoriety for offending some crackpot American church.

Two days later, at the same crematorium, it had been Wendy's turn. Don had wept, Becky had wept, David had tried to be stoic and failed, and Nina had broken down even more profoundly than she'd expected to, quite unable to be the strong person everyone took her for. When it was over she could think of only one thing beyond her guilt at having provided the setting for her sister's destruction: to see Will. Will had been there for so many years, during all their tribulations, money worries, occasional health problems and so on, yet he wasn't there now, supporting her in her grief; a grief he would share, for he'd been fond of Wendy. Doubting that he'd heard about the killing from any other source, she'd written to him, telling him about it, but she'd seen the way he treated mail that came through the door at Bleakridge and guessed that he hadn't even noticed a letter from her. She'd tried several times to get through to the pub to leave a message for him, but the only number available for The Duck and Whippet was a landline, and whenever she'd called it was either engaged or no one picked up. No answerphone either, no voicemail. There might have been other ways to get word to him, other numbers to ring – a police station in the vicinity perhaps – but she hadn't tried, hadn't really considered such ways. Which left only one.

But she couldn't leave the children immediately after the funeral, especially the completely broken Becky, and had waited until now to drive North. With tears in her eyes much of the way, she had just one objective in mind. To reach Will. No thought as to what might happen after that. Just to get to him, tell him, exchange griefs.

79

There was one picture that caught Colin's eye more than all the others. It was one of the larger ones, nearly as tall as him, and even though it seemed badly painted he couldn't help feeling that it might come to life any second. It might or might not have been of the same woman. The hair was longer in this, all tangled, and she was starkers, just standing there, full frontal, surrounded by clumsy gobs of paint that he guessed were meant to be trees. And that look of hers. Those eyes, staring right at him. He felt that if he blinked she might lean out and touch him. Drag him into the picture.

A sudden sound outside. Car pulling into the yard. He forgot about the picture, forgot everything except that he shouldn't be there. He raced to the kitchen, to the window behind the sink by which he used to gain entry. He wrestled with the catch. Couldn't shift it. Now what? Where can I hide? Not the bathroom. Could be trapped in there. Upstairs is all there is. Either that I just stand here waiting to be caught, reported to Dad, given a whack or a mouthful.

He ran upstairs as quietly as he could. Reached the top, and a choice of two rooms, the main bedroom or the smaller room across from it, nothing more than a box-room really. The box-room was the obvious choice, but the door was closed. He tried the handle. It squealed as he turned it. Rather than turn it further he tiptoed into the open-doored bedroom, praying that the floor wouldn't creak as he slid beneath the unmade bed. It did, but only once. It was dusty under there. He lay face down on the bare boards, in the dust, hoping he wouldn't sneeze.

80

Nina called his name. No answer, but the door wasn't closed. Pushing it back, about to call again, she was met with the same sight, or sights, that had startled Colin minutes earlier. Like him, she stared from picture to picture, but in something close to horror, for she was clearly the subject of many of them, distorted, warped, abused, her body savaged, sundered, twisted.

81

The day, cool and melancholy, was fading. Billy paused, boots lodged in furrows in the uncompromising earth; gazed across the gnarled slope of the land wondering, as he did so often, what the point of all this was. Survival? For what? For Ella, who cared so little for him? Ella despised him, he had no doubt of it now. Her every word and gesture showed it, proved it. And she made a fool of him at every opportunity, whenever there was a man about. Man or youth. His forebears would have sneered at him for putting up with such behavior. Even his mother would have told him to get his head together about Ella. He could barely coax a living for one out of the hill, let alone two, and the woman who shared his home had no respect for him, no loyalty, love. He looked about him. All this, for nothing. His life, for nothing. Ella, for nothing. It was all he could do not to break down.

He did not break down.

He dropped his tools, left them where they fell. Tomorrow was another day. Just one more like today. What little there was could wait.

He started up the hill.

82

A spot of idle chat with Harry and a couple of village men, and with just two halves of something local inside him Will headed back. On the track, a little way from the top of the hill, he paused, short of breath. *My God, if I still smoked I'd be in even worse condition.* Reaching the yard, he paused again, for a different reason. A car was parked there, his car, their car, his and Nina's. But then, quite suddenly, it wasn't their car. Wasn't any car. It was an old farm cart with big wooden wheels. There was also an ancient water pump that hadn't been there before, and... and both were gone, and the house shifted uneasily, as if uncertain which phase of its existence to offer. One instant it was the ordinary present-day house, the next the pitiful near-ruin he'd known as a boy, and then... then it was the simple dwelling of an earlier day that his imagination had built in some of his paintings.

He advanced slowly into the yard. Chickens scattered. Then there were no chickens. The old cart returned, but was immediately replaced by a toppling midden. Then there was no midden but a rain barrel beneath a drainpipe from guttering around the roof. Then the barrel was gone, and for a moment there was decay and ruination, but in half a trice: new paintwork, then plain stone and twisting ivy, until these too were supplanted, by primroses in window boxes. He'd never seen window boxes at Bleakridge.

Above all this, the sky shifted as rapidly and willfully as the generations of the house. Clouds fled and doubled back, the seasons too, with increasing rapidity. Standing there, a mere observer, it was hard to tell if he'd just experienced day, night, winter, high summer, snowfall, storm, so fleeting were all of these. One second, black skies sagged against an adequate roof, the next the building was a moldering shell with a dazzle of sunlight projected from above. There was rain on his cheeks, and he shivered in a blast of cold air, and heat prickled his skin, and he stood on hard mud, then wet slush, then mud again, and the door was closed, and yet it wasn't.

He moved closer to the house, hesitantly, nervously, and when he placed his hand on the door it seemed to move, but at the same time it did not. Then it was a different door. And different again. Back and forth, forth and back, new door, old door, fallen door, fresh paint, bare oak, heavy grain, then, beyond the door, the room he'd left so recently was one he hadn't set foot in for a quarter of a century, and there was graffiti on the walls, and rubble and weeds underfoot, and then the floor was bare, and the walls clean and color-washed, and there was an old tea chest, and a big armchair with its stuffing hanging out, and a hand-carved stool, and there were logs in the hearth, slabs of peat smoldering, a black-leaded range nearby, and in the center of the room a solid-looking table which she leant back on, her upper body and head shrouded in shadow, and then everything slowed, and settled, and lingered, and she continued to lean back, supporting herself with the heels of her hands, and he stood at the open door, exploring the spread of her legs, the V at the top in the weave of that unfamiliar skirt, and he could think of nothing but the body underneath. The skin. The flesh.

83

Beneath the bed, a gap in the dusty floorboards provided a partial view of the room below. The view did not ease Colin's mind. The woman was back and he was up here, in her bedroom. A sudden sound down there. He angled his head, his eye, saw that the writer or whatever he was had come in. *That's all I need, two of them. If they come up I've had it.*

But it didn't look as if they planned to come up just yet. She'd parked her backside on the edge of the table and pulled her skirt up past her knees, her thighs, and Jesus, she wasn't wearing anything underneath. He peered more intently. He'd never seen one of those before, not in real life. The man moved closer, unclasped his belt, dropped his trousers and pants. The woman slid her legs apart, wide apart, and he shuffled between them, wriggled about a bit, pushed himself in. Colin's mouth went dry. The woman leant back further, her long bare legs looping around the man's lower back as he rammed her slowly, repeatedly, repeatedly.

84

In the yard, Billy walked round his cart to the old water pump, gripped the handle. Gripped it but did not carry the motion through. Noises. From the house. He tilted his head. Listened. Ella's voice. Sounded like she was in pain. He approached. The door was open, just a bit, indistinct movements in the gloom within. He squinted to sharpen the image. And saw. Saw all that he needed to, and much more than he wished to.

She wasn't in pain.

His chest heaved. He closed his eyes. There were tears when he opened them. He shook them away. Did she *have* to leave the door open? Didn't she care at *all* if he saw? The worst of it was the way she held the man, legs encircling him as if to hold him in place, make sure he didn't let up til she was satisfied. She was in control. The incomer was nothing more than the latest poor dupe. No different from the others, merely older. Not his fault, or theirs really. It was Ella's. Ella knew what she wanted and was damn well going to get it. She was in charge.

But no. No, he couldn't blame her, not entirely. It was

this place. This fucking hill. Fucking house. Bleakridge. Their brooding, pitiless combination fostered and spurred all the misery, humiliation, hopelessness. Ella was merely their living instrument.

He took a breath. Then another. A long, slow breath.

Their *living* instrument...

He watched the rutting couple with something akin to grief. *Enough of that, please Ella, please my love, do stop, for me.* In the room, half in shadow, she turned her head. Saw him in the doorway. Carried right on, her heels now riding the man's bare pumping arse.

Billy stifled a sob, then threw his head back, and roared, simply roared.

And charged.

85

From where Colin lay, eye to the crack in the floorboards, Billy, whose name he didn't know, whom he'd never seen before, filled the doorway, arms raised above his head as if to pull the house down around them all. Then he was running in, bellowing nothing that made any sense, gripping the man by the collar, lugging him to the door, hurling him out, like rubbish. Returning, he gripped the woman's arm, hauled her off the table, then caught her by the hair, began spinning her round by it, round and round and round.

Colin, above all this, could only stare, riveted by the unfolding drama. He saw Billy whirling the woman by her hair, heard her yells and shrieks as her legs and feet and arms bashed anything that got in the way. Then he let go of her, quite suddenly, perhaps losing his grip, and she skidded across the floor. But he wasn't done yet. He rushed forward, seized her by the ankles, began swinging her again, round and round, round and round, and this time it was her head that struck one thing after another, the edge of the open door, the walls, the table, everything, shouting, shrieking, bawling. The whole house seemed to shake.

But soon the woman's cries turned into funny little whimpers. Bang, crash, whimper, crack, whimper, whimper, and then she was making no sound at all, and Billy stopped whizzing her round and round. He set her down on the floor, bent over her, saw what a mess the house had made of her face, her hair, and he howled, howled dementedly, and ran out, leaving her where she lay, all twisted and battered, all bloody. Quite still.

Colin waited for what felt like an age before easing out from the bed. He dashed dust from his face, stifled a sneeze, crept downstairs. He paused at the foot of the stairs; looked into the room. In spite of all the crashing and thumping and whirling, almost everything was as it had been before. The skull that he'd vaguely noticed on the mantelpiece now lay against one of the table legs, but none of the paintings had fallen over or even been knocked. The model for many of the pictures – her or someone very like her – lay on the floor. Her skirt wasn't bunched around her hips any more. Pity.

He went to the door. The man who'd been chucked outside was still there, sprawling, trousers and pants round his ankles. His eyes were closed. Fearing the return of the lunatic who'd done this to these two, Colin went to the fence, looked over and down, across, this way, that. Nothing. No one. Maybe he was round the other side, of the hill or the house. His first thought, now, was to climb over the fence and run and skid and roll down the hill as fast as he could; but he hesitated. Looked back at the house. He went to the nearest corner of the building and peered round it. The nutter wasn't there. He crept to the next corner. Not there either. And the next – not there – and back to the front yard. The man still lay on the ground. He still wasn't moving. Colin looked in the door. The woman hadn't moved either. The house, like this couple who'd taken it over, was utterly still. And in the stillness, a thought came. An opportunity.

If I can't have it, why should anyone else?

He went inside, to the table, littered with paints, tools, rubbish. Among all this, a box of matches. He took a match out. Struck it. It snapped in two, unlit. He tried another, with more success. He cupped it, and, nursing the small flame in his palms, carried it to one of the awful paintings. He held the flame to the canvas. A small sizzle, a pause, then the flame spread a little, and a little more, and the painting caught fire in a modest sort of way. He went to the door. From there he watched the flame reach another painting and start to pass across it.

As he left the house it started to rain.

86

The rain woke him. He opened his eyes – and winced. His back, where he'd landed. He became aware of the hard ground beneath him. Looked about him. No iron pump, no chickens or cart. The car was there. Which meant Nina was. What was it Mr. Morley said, according to Harry Sewell? Something about things being changeable at Bleakridge, all mixed up. He couldn't argue with that.

He started to rise, but stumbled, as if his ankles were tied together. They were, in a way. He pulled his pants and trousers up. Was buckling his belt when he smelt smoke. He went to the door of the house, peered into a gloom minimally illuminated by small flames. Then he saw her, on the floor, lying awkwardly. He went inside.

'Nina. Nina.'

She stirred. Flinched to see him leaning over her.

'Are you all right?' he asked.

'I don't know, what happened?'

'You tell me.'

'Did I pass out or something?'

'If you did, I didn't see.'

She sat up. 'In my head we were... you and me...'

She glanced at the table, littered with painting and drawing materials. He said nothing. She started to get up, too quickly, sat down again. He offered his hand. She took it. Hauled herself to her feet. Only then did she realize.

'Christ, the place is on fire.'

'Just the pictures, I think,' he said.

'The house'll catch too. We have to do something.'

'Like what? We're not a fire brigade.'

They watched the flames creep from painting to painting. Just the paintings. Whenever they touched parts of the house, or things that belonged to it, they guttered out or retreated, moved on to another picture.

'All these paintings,' Nina murmured.

'I've been busy,' he said.

'You set fire to them?'

'Not me.'

'Well they didn't light themselves.'

They continued to watch as the pictures, one by one, were blackened or consumed by the slow, almost disinterested flames.

'You don't seem too bothered,' she said after a while.

'They don't matter. They're out of me now.'

'Some of them...' She glanced at him. 'Of me?'

'Just pictures,' he said.

'So, what, we're just going to stand here watching them burn?'

'Seems as good a plan as any.'

Silence between them for a further while, until Nina said: 'Did you get my letter?'

He looked at her. 'Letter?'

'Yes, about...'

She stopped. His blankness answered her question. Or did it? Either he hadn't seen the letter about Wendy or he'd been too wrapped up in himself, all this, these pictures, to be stirred by its contents.

In the moments it took Nina's mind to formulate these alternatives, Will's own was filled once again with the image of her riding that man with such complete, absorbed, blissful abandon on their living room floor.

Giving him the benefit of the doubt, the other being unthinkable, Nina attempted to put the event, the tragedy, the loss, into words.

'Will, there's something I have to tell you.'

She faltered, unable to come out with it just like that.

But he'd heard enough. He knew where this was going. The big confession. An admission of the extracurricular shagging, a long-term fling perhaps, that he'd be expected to absorb, accommodate, forgive because it was offered here and now rather than be stumbled upon or realized at some later date. The bitterness flooded back. The anger. Forgive? No. Never. In that moment it was all he could do not to lash out, send her flying.

'Forget it,' he said. 'I don't give a shit.'

And, unable to bear her company, presence, proximity, he stepped away from her, turned about, crossed the room, stormed out of the house, leaving her staring after him, stunned by his reaction – so he *had* read the letter – appalled by his lack of feeling, his callousness.

Outside, half way across the yard, Will paused. Where now? *What* now? He had no idea, but he couldn't stay here. The rain was heavier than it had been, but he didn't hurry down the track. By the time he reached the spinney his clothes were soaked. He sought shelter beneath the trees. Above him, way above, rooks shuffled in their nests.

In a minute he heard the car coming down the hill. Then it was on the stretch of track he stood beside. Nina, at the wheel, stared straight ahead, determined not to see him, and then she was gone, and the rain eased off.

'Colin? Colin!'

Along the track, Harry Sewell calling for his boy. Will looked around. No sign of the kid. He looked again toward Harry, but Harry was heading back to the village.

He stepped out from the trees, but stumbled, and in the stumbling blinked, and he was in a boat, a rowing boat, and there were kids there, three of them, no, four, he was the fourth, and he was going to fall in the water and drown, but then, change of scene and year and he was in a fleeting succession of flats, rooms, bathrooms, all ages, all bodies, once a haunted figure in a painting, then sprawling naked and Inger... I mean Lena... no, Nina, crouching, lifts her head, laughing as a mouthful of jizz spills between her lips, slops down her chin. 'My favorite pastime,' I confess. 'Mine too,' she says, and then she's gone, jizz and all, laugh and all, taking our past with her, and I'm fleetingly bereft, and walking past ruined cottages which, as I go by, rebuild themselves, and there are people leaning on garden walls, and a very tall man with wild hair and a beak of a nose winks at me, and for a moment, just a mo, it all makes sense, all the shit makes sense, but it passes, as ever, as always, the nonsense returns, resumes, and I'm in a sunlit patch of existence between shadows and I'm everyone rolled into one – he, she, they, them, I, me, uppity-duppity – wondering what the fuck's real and what isn't and if it matters anyway in a melting universe of selective interpretation, off-kilter recall, delusional disorder, cognitive dissonance, and I'm strolling through a graveyard where headstones bear the wrong names and dates, and now I'm back on the hill, leaning out, and down there the circle of miniliths falls back and the earth they encircle rises, and there he is, the Mississippi bible-thumper, or maybe the farmer or whatever he is, pointing a fleshless finger, or a gun, and light-moments later I'm elsewhere, elsewhen. Being at all of these points successively or concurrently is a relief of sorts, so far are they from the frustrations, disappointments and rages that lie in wait. But even with all that, all this, if I could choose a day, an age, a place, what would it be, where would I – ?

An overhead squawk; sharp, irritable, insistent. He

looked up. One squawker but many a rookish eye stared down at him, as though awaiting a commitment, to year, to place, to age. He closed his eyes, as if to ponder this, decide.

'Come along, Will, teatime!'

He looked out. Along the track. And slowly nodded, and stepped out from this space, this wooded place, where generations of rooks have massed, and I'm walking, head uncovered, grateful for the feel of rain on skin because getting soaked by rain is better than non-existence, where nothing's felt, seen, heard, discovered, and away I go, obedient as ever with my grandparents if not my dad, and a few paces on the rain stops completely, suddenly, and sun splashes my world and I'm dry, my clothes and hair are dry, and 'S'all mixed up, Gramps,' I say, reaching him.

'What's that, lad?'

'Nothing. Nothing.'

'Better get a move on,' his grandfather said. 'Be in trouble if we don't. You know what the old girl's like about her perishing meals.'

And together we walk to the village, his old man hand on my young boy shoulder, and I've never felt more sane, so 'right', in time, in place. In life.

87

That night Billy wrapped Ella in a blanket from their bed and carried her gently to the flat piece of ground just below the fence – the little garden his mother and grandmother used to grow herbs and flowers in – and buried her there, right in the middle. He sobbed as he rearranged the turf over her, whispering 'My love, my love,' over and over. Returning to the house, too sad to do anything but sleep, he settled down on the floor by the fireplace, as he had so many nights of late. The fire was out.

When he woke early next morning his head was full of Ella. Lines came to him, the opening lines of a poem, a new poem, celebrating their...

But then he recalled his rage of yesterday, and the grief that followed it, the face last seen smashed beyond recognition, the lovely hair matted and tangled, and he cried out in agony, anguish, despair.

'Ella! My love! My sweet girl!'

When he felt sufficiently able, he went to 'the place', as he'd already begun to think of it, and stood over it, alternately staring down and closing his eyes. Once, opening his eyes, he staggered, for there, all about him, were figures, almost-figures, featureless, ranged in a circle, facing him, as if judging him. But then he blinked, and there were no almost-figures, no judges, and he was alone again, sagging with grief, and the horror of what he'd done to his beloved.

In each of the days that followed he went to where Ella lay, and he stood there, over her, imagining how things could have been, should have been. If there were any further manifestations of featureless figures he didn't see them, keeping his head down, whispering to Ella, always Ella.

One afternoon he stood at the door of the house looking out across the cluttered, disarrayed yard, thinking of those who'd stood there before him. Granny Flo, his dad, Mama, little Sal, and now it was just him, wifeless, childless, the last Rainey of Bleakridge. The loneliest too, no doubt. He didn't want to be alone again. Not here. Not here. Thinking this, he turned around as if to take in the house's interior; assess its worth as a dwelling to pass months and years in, to slowly age in, alone, and in the turning his gaze took in the stairs, the four that could be seen from there, and the sight of them, the very familiar, easily dismissed sight at other times, his memory of other stairs was jogged, and the old house they belonged to, in the woods of the training valley in Dorset, where he'd met the angry youth who claimed to have lived there once. Those stairs had reminded him of these, of Bleakridge, and here he was today, *at* Bleakridge, reminded of that old house, and the day he went there, as if the two were somehow linked and held by a twitchy, uneasy rope of reality.

And now he recalled something else seen in that sad, neglected house: the patch of wall where the wallpaper had peeled or been torn away. The 'graffiti wall'. It wasn't the scribbles or rhymes or smut that he thought of now, but the crudely-etched drawing of a man hanging from a gibbet, and with this memory, his situation, the thankless, unprofitable, lonely life ahead of him settled into place in his mind as the only outcome there could be for him. He sighed. And sighed again. No, he thought, no, no, no, I won't have it, it can't be, and he went to the stairs, and climbed slowly, heavily, to the bedroom loft.

When he came down minutes later, he wore the second-hand suit from the market. In his hand he carried the yellow tie also bought that day. His wedding tie. He dragged a chair from the table and got up onto it. He found a small gap between the ceiling and the central beam that supported it, forced the tie through, pulled it, looped it round the beam with room to spare, knotted it tightly. He inserted his head in the loop and settled it round his neck, his head pressed awkwardly against the beam. Because of the angle, the room was peculiarly tilted, but from where he stood on the chair he could see out into the yard, where his few undernourished chickens pecked hopefully at the ground. They wouldn't find much. The sky, gray and heavy today, hung about the hill like a shroud. There was a storm in the air.

'Oh, Ella,' he murmured, and again, 'Ella,' intending her name to be his last word.

He was about to kick the chair away when he heard a dog barking in the near distance. He listened, listened hard, the raised grain of the old oak grazing his temple. Another bark. Jess, he thought. It's Jess, I know it, Jess, home at last. Overjoyed, he struggled to loosen the tie, but in his haste his foot slipped, the chair toppled sideways, and he fell, neck still enclosed by the tightly-knotted loop. The breath spurted from him. 'Jess!' he tried to shout, but couldn't.

From where he hung by the neck he looked toward the no-longer-tilted doorway. Jess wasn't there and the only sound was a dense rushing, like water drumming in his ears. A moment of struggling panic, but then calm. It has to be, has to be. The wedding tie cut into his neck. His eyes felt that they would burst. He tried to bring his eyelids down, but couldn't. And it was then that a thought came. The box. The Poetry Box. All my writings. My personal lines. No one must find them, see them. But he couldn't get down. Couldn't shift the so-tight loop in the tie.

The room swayed. Walls converged. The ceiling opened out. His tongue filled his mouth like a potato.

88

The house sighed. Moved on from Billy's day. Fell into disrepair. Kids broke in, drew and wrote and pissed on the walls. In time, eventually, it was partially rebuilt, modernized after a fashion, and a newly retired couple bought it, went to live there. But there was something about the place. Something that troubled them but was hard to pin down, and sometimes... sometimes they could swear things were different there, fleetingly. The couple left, but others came, and rented it, a man and woman in their late thirties, and their Bleakridge story began. Their very brief story. Then they too went, and no one else moved in, and the house again deteriorated. The odd curious hill climber wondered about the place's history. Also about the circle of standing stones on the scrap of overgrown ground below the fallen fence. Some noticed that bits of the stones were coming away but didn't look closely. Like the house, there was something about those featureless figures that did not encourage loiterers.

Once more, Bleakridge became a wretched shell of a place, roof open to the sky, all weathers, all seasons;

crumbling walls, graffiti-rich between scrambling mantels of ivy, front door kicked in, windows squeezed out or smashed. Nothing else. A transitory shadow now and then, the odd shiver, that's all.

And silence.

Such silence.

Such depthless, heartfelt silence.

THE SILENCE OF BLEAKRIDGE
is part of a three-novel sequence.
The other two are:

THIS RUINED PLACE
THE RAINEY SEASONS

These three may be read singly or in any order, as stand-alone books. The main link between them is individuals by the name of Rainey, connections which some of them are unaware of. While set in different locations at different points in time, each book contains small nudges to the other two which the interested reader might be pleased to discover.